To Mary Ann
Blessings—

IN A TWINKLING

IN A TWINKLING

THE LAST MAN TAKEN

RANDALL JOHNSON

Published by Randall Johnson

Contents

Contents		v
Introduction: *Charlie Randall*		8
1	Monday - The Dreams Begin	10
2	Tuesday – Rose and Jon	16
3	Later Tuesday – Arlington Cemetery	20
4	Wednesday– Old Men Dream Dreams	24
5	Thursday – Finding Faith	31
6	Friday –Pastor Doug Kucher	40
7	Saturday– A Sermon Rewritten	51
8	Sunday – Dreams of Peace	56
9	The Sermon	59
10	Monday – Viral Sermon / The Team	67
11	Tuesday – WW Vision / Time Crunch	74
12	Wednesday - Preparations	78
13	Thursday–Final Details / Charlie's Dilemma	83
14	Friday – Final Details	90

15 Worldwide 93

16 In A Twinkling 103

This book is dedicated to
My Lovely Wife, Cindy
&
Our Courageous Son, Kole

Copyright 2021 by Randall S. Johnson

All rights reserved. No part of this book may be used or reproduced by any means, graphic, electronic o mechanical, including photocopying, recording, taping, or any information storage retrieval system without the written permission of the publisher except in the case of brief quotations embodied in critical articles or reviews.

Because of the dynamic nature of the nature, any web addresses or links contained in this book may have changed since publication and may no longer be valid.

ISBN: 979-8-9859130- 0-2 (SC)
ISBN: 979-8-9859130-1-9 (HC)
ISBN: 979-8-9859130-2-6 (E)

BISAC FIC027000; REL030000; REL067060

Library of Congress Control Number: 2022904489
Rev. 03-16-2022
Published by RS Johnson Publishers in Rochester, NY
Cover design by Randall Johnson

Epigraph

"Two Men will be in the field, one will be taken and the other left."
Matthew 24:40 (NIV)

"Listen, I tell you a mystery: We will not all sleep, but we will all be changed in a flash, in a tinkling of an eye."
1 COR 15:51 (NIV)

Preface

Indecision is a trait we all must have to one degree or another. Sometimes this is a good thing such as when deciding to marry someone or whether to take a job offer in a different city, getting all the facts necessary to make a good decision takes time and necessitates a modicum of indecision. Sometimes indecision is a bad thing with undesirable consequences such as waiting too long to marry someone, perhaps 'the' someone, and she moves on without you or not taking that out-of-town job only to find out it was given to someone else and then discover you will get laid off from your present one at the end of the week.

Quite often, in the spiritual sense, waiting to commit to an invitation to become a Christian with associated lifestyle changes becomes a decision that can be faced down the road, usually when you are in a different situation that makes the eventual change more attractive if not acceptable. Maybe this is when you find out you have cancer, or your parent dies and that starts you thinking of your own mortality. Maybe then you can commit to becoming a Christian and believing and putting your trust in Jesus. Maybe your current lifestyle conflicts with the teachings of a Christian faith, such as an affair you are in, or your taxes are too high, and you are fudging a bit, or you are over-indulging in the sauce with no intention to stop. Such things are not acceptable behavior, and you are just not quite ready to give them up. So, a decision becomes an indecision, and you kick the can down the road.

What happens if there is no more road to kick a can down? Your five to ten or twenty-year cushion of time for such decisions suddenly shrinks to a few months, or days or even hours. Surely then you will have the opportunity to make a rational decision – or perhaps you may become filled with anger at a God that is robbing you of your deserved multi-year dithering plan in which case you vacillate and fret. Or worse yet, your "decision cushion" shrinks to a few seconds or its instantaneous such as in a murder or a heart-attack or a traffic accident. There would be no time to make your decision and then your life ends and then what? Your indecision will become a decision and you will be betting your eternity that your indecision was a good choice.

Dithering in life's decisions is what this book is about. Not deciding what to do spiritually is where we find Jon Wyatt in his mid-sixties. He has been a pastor at a straightlaced denominational church in Arlington, Virginia for over thirty-five years and he is comfortable in his career, his lifestyle, his friends, his work, his marriage, and his spirituality. Comfortable. Yes, amazingly comfortable but dangerous. Life can be extremely dangerous sitting on a cushion.

(As a personal note, I too as an author, need to stop dithering get on with writing this book).

PART ONE: THE CALLING

Introduction: Charlie Randall

First let me say I am skeptical. I am proud of my journalistic standing within the investigative news media. I am fair and I ask hard questions. I try to turn-over all the stones, get to the bottom of issues, explore hidden agendas, reveal truth.

Although my talents are better utilized within the criminal realm, I have been assigned this project with limited lead time to complete my findings and submit my report to Pastor Kucher. The deadline, though short, is of no concern to me since I have a strong incentive from another publisher to begin work on their assignment. My report will be in early, and I will be free to move on.

The only reason I have taken on this assignment is pastor Doug Kucher is a long-time friend of my father and as a favor to Dad I am taking on this endeavor. So, I will begin with all the professional and nonjudgmental attitude I can muster and conduct the interview I have been assigned.

Charlie Randall, Journalist, & Investigative Reporter

~~~

Background before my Saturday appointment with Jon: Arlington, Virginia is a bedroom community for the hordes of governmental workers and lobbyists of all sorts and types. It is an affluent suburb of the DC metropolitan area and personifies the perception of sophisticated snobbery. If you talk about religion in this area, you will be summarily dismissed as one of "those" people who are relegated to the masses and are quite apart and below the enlightened intelligentsia who pervade the bastions of the DC higher society. A Presbyterian church fits well within this realm as it suits a need to appear 'religious' while feigning commitment to its purpose.

Here I met Jon Wyatt, Pastor of the First Presbyterian Church of Arlington quietly fulfilling all the trappings and airs of the societal neighborhood, all the while preaching a word, little noticed and soon forgotten.

My appointment with Jon was in his office on Saturday. He had just completed his sermon for the next day and was eager to see me and recount his past week. A week that he indicated had changed his life forever. The following is his story…

1

Monday - The Dreams Begin

Everything seemed slightly out of focus, I am standing in a field stretching far off to the horizon. The landscape is generally flat with long gentle slopes, not really hills. Straight in front of me in the far distance is a wall. At least that is what I would guess to call it, yes, it seems like a wall.

~~~

Jon awoke with a sudden jolt and a cold sweat. Confused, with his mind slowly clearing the cobwebs of a deep sleep from his thoughts, the memory of his dream was beginning to fade. He was determined to concentrate on the dream that had so vividly invaded his sleep. He reached over to his nightstand and flipped on the lamp instantly dispelling the darkness and revealing the familiarity of his bedroom surroundings – nothing had changed, everything was still in the same place it was when he laid his head on his pillow hours ago.

Rose was still deeply asleep and motionless beside him, the digital clock quietly displayed 3:16 AM as Jon began to assess exactly what had happened. His dream seemed so real and yet it was also too simple. His mind ached to recall any details of what he had experienced and all he could recollect was him standing in a wheat field, it was daytime, and, in the far distance, a supposed wall stretched to the horizon. That was it. That was all he could pull from his brain.

He sat up on the side of the bed and tried to put into context the dream and how significant it was since he had never in his life seen a wall like that, which now haunted his memory, and the field in which he stood was another experience he could say for sure was not from his past life. Yet the dream left him with an ominous feeling of significance. Still, the lack of any details, other than a simple image, contradicted the strange emotion he felt. Sensing a lack of insight to tackle the analysis at this time of the early morning, he yielded to the ache in his brain for more sleep and he fell back into the pillow and the comfort of his bed. His thoughts drifted back into the quiet of the night.

~~~

The comforting aroma of coffee and frying bacon permeated their small bungalow. Jon always arose long before Rose would make her appearance at the breakfast table. Every hair had its place, and the simple makeup was always conservative and proper as befitting the wife of a prominent pastor. It was a Monday, same as just about every other Monday.

"Morning Hon." offered Jon breaking the silence as he placed a cup of coffee in front of Rose's place at the kitchen table. "Did you sleep well?"

"Jon, I slept like a baby last night. As soon as my head hit the pillow my brain switched off and I was in la-la land. Mmmm the bacon smells good this morning, and do we still have any of that delicious orange juice? Another morning without that delicious juice and I might just blah, blah, blah, blah …

Jon was waiting for it and as soon as she took a breath he inserted "I slept well but had a strange dream."

"As I was saying, Amy surely could have just about any man on that campus, but she just seems to be settling, you know? Settling, that's what kids do now days is settle. Their lifelong standards go out the window as soon as they unpack at college. I swear this next generation will surely go to pot, and I do not mean marijuana, before they reach forty. And speaking of marijuana ......" Rose's voice trailed off in Jon's brain as the conversation drifted away in meaningless significance.

Finally, grabbing his keys and coat, Jon interrupted "Well, I'm off to see Jerry this morning. He wants to talk to me about our financial advisor. He is retiring and he wants to check around before he settles on the next guy in the office. Be back after lunch."

Rose offered "OK dear. Let me know later what your dream was." It seemed to placate Jon that she had heard his response. She made a mental note to follow-up with him later at diner.

~~~

The ten-minute ride to Jerry's job at the Costco construction site was uneventful and Jon spotted Jerry walking out of the construction office trailer with a fist full of papers and wearing his yellow hard hat a little tilted to the right. That was Jerry, always a little out of kilter. With a short-wave Jerry acknowledged Jon and shot out "Be there in five, I have to see to something first."

Jon knew Jerry since they were in Junior High at Saint Mary's Parochial School of the Blessed Sacrament. They grew up together through high school competing in all the sports. Jerry was the star athlete, gifted with great genes for such endeavors, while Jon was the cerebral one keeping the bench warm and gained exclusive experience in mopping up games when the Saints were ahead by twenty or more points. They had a million laughs over the years and even shed a few silent manly tears as well. They were tight and shared their lives freely, always leaving out intimate details of course. Jon went off to seminary school at eighteen and Jerry, short for Jeremiah, went to Virginia Tech. They drifted apart until after graduation where they both re-settled in Arlington, their hometown now for over forty years.

Jerry approached Jon after a few minutes. "Sorry about that, we had a crisis over some delivery of roofing materials that was backordered and just arrived today. I had to see the delivery was quickly unloaded and the crew started work immediately. How's it going Jon?'

"Great Jerry, things are quiet as usual. Rose is fine and looking forward to having lunch with your Betty today. They do seem to never run out of something to say. I could never quite figure out how they do that."

"One of life's mysteries. Way too complex for us to understand. Say Jon, I was wondering if you would mind if I reached out to your and Rose's financial advisor. Mine is retiring and I am not sure I want my future to be in the hands of a young college graduate still wet behind his ears. I guess I just want someone who has a lot of experience managing my life's savings. Are you and Rose satisfied with your guy?"

"Well, my GUY, is a lady and she is doing right well with us. We seem to have enough set aside to be able to retire in a couple of years although I am not quite sure why I would do that since I make a good living as a pastor at Arlington Presbyterian, I get a new car every three years – to make my rounds you know, and they also add money to my 401K every month. The work is not hard, and I get plenty of time off – just need to be there on Sundays and special occasions.

"Her name is Elaine Smithfield and I'll text you, her number. Tell her I sent you, it might get you a pen or one of her calendars."

"Sure, thing Jon, Thanks!"

"By the way Jerry, I had the strangest dream last night. Kind of left me with a sense of ominous importance, strange as that may seem."

"Go on."

"Well, it was such a simple dream and yet I am particularly puzzled about it. Usually, my dreams are about keeping a tiny sunfish afloat in storm-raged ocean or trying to find my way home from an unknown city but this one was different and even caused me to feel an ominous sense of danger and intrigue.

"There I was, standing in a field, it was daytime I guess since I could see my surroundings. The field stretched off to the horizon in all directions and there was this wall, as clearly as I can remember there was a wall, far off in the distance and disappearing to the horizon. Then I woke up. That was it. That's all there was to the dream."

"It sounds to me that you are a bit preoccupied with your dream." Jerry added, "Just let it go, dreams are just your brain playing back old memories and trying to reset itself."

"You may be right Jerry. Hey, are we still on for dinner this Thursday? Rose has found a great recipe for beef barbeque that you and Betty will love. See you around seven?"

"Yeah, seven." Jerry replied as he grabbed his walkie-talkie and barked out some orders while shuffling up to the trailer again.

The rest of the day came and went in the all too typical routine of a pastor: A few phone calls, stop by the office, and a quick visit to the hospital to comfort the children of an octogenarian, a long-time church member, on life support after decades of smoking. Mental note: a funeral will be necessary sometime next week.

At dinner Rose was all news from her luncheon with the "ladies" and Jon was all ears waiting for her to mention his dream, but the subject never came up, so Jon just let it go. It probably wasn't that important anyway; it was only a dream. So, what! Just forget about it.

The usual drivel was on the tube and Jon became bored with the lack of substance in the banal sit-com. Rose seemed to be entertained and Jon delved into his latest Jon Grisham novel as the evening hours drifted away. At 10:30 he arose from his reading chair and announced he was tired and was heading for bed. "Goodnight honey" he whispered in Rose's ear as he kissed her on the cheek.

"Good night! I will be there in a few minutes when this show is over. Love you!"

2

Tuesday – Rose and Jon

Rose was still deep asleep at 9:00 AM, unaware of Jon's mysterious nocturn adventure. Her dreams were filled with "to-do" list items and replaying conversations of social doings with the church ladies, all important in framing her anticipated activities of the new day.

Rose slowly awoke to the wafting breath of a breeze emanating from the kitchen carrying the instantly familiar and welcome aroma of Old Spice cologne that Jon has been wearing for years. It seems her entire sense of affection, devotion and dedication to Jon was triggered by that simple yet elegant fragrance and, without consciousness of thought, Rose was transported back to her memories of their courting days.

Rose met Jon at a high-school dance after a basketball game and instantly fell in 'like' with him. Jon was a nice guy but not overwhelming in his persona. He had a chauvinistic attitude and liked to drink, both red warning flags in Rose's book but she saw something in Jon, call it potential or what have you, but Jon had caught Rosie's eye and they went out on a couple of dates. Nothing much became of the relationship and Jon soon headed off to college. He ended up at Edwards Theology in Cambridge more as an after-thought. He was struggling between a career in social services and the ministry so he flipped a coin and social service won out except he could not start his major studies for an extra semester, so he took the introductory course for Theology and just kept going. Studies were relatively easy, and he figured he could find his calling in either field. At Edwards he became a prodigal of sorts, heading out into the night life and caving into his fleshly desires while keeping up with his studies – sort of a Jekyll and Hyde existence.

Jon came home to visit Rose toward the end of his first semester. It became all too evident Jon had changed during his time away and 'changed' in a bad way. Rose gave him the ultimatum of 'shape up or ship out', she just was not going to wait for him if his new lifestyle became his life's ambition.

Apparently, Jon went back to school and thought about their relationship and decided "with her" was what he wanted and "without her" was not an option. Before Rose knew it, Jon showed up at her doorstep all cleaned up and wearing Old Spice. The rest, as they say, is history.

~~~

Jon couldn't wait for Rose to awaken. As usual he was up early, showered and shaved. "Morning Dear, I have something to tell you."

"I could smell your cologne all the way back in the bedroom and just had to follow my nose out here." Rose said as she arrived for breakfast, dressed, and preened as usual. "How are you this morning?" she continued as she fixed her coffee, black with French-vanilla cream. Now, at this point Rose would begin a monologue for the next hour or so that would cover all the usual topics and maybe a few more that would pop into her brain, all cross-referenced and categorized to emphasize her opinions of the world. But the lingering effects of the Old Spice seemed to throw Rose off her script for the moment and Jon had a chance to grab hold of the conversation.

"Now I need you to listen to me. I have had a dream each of the last two nights that have been curiously ominous yet baffling in meaning and I want you to her me out."

Jon then told her about the first dream and then the second –

"Everything seems a bit clearer this time. I am standing in a vast field covered with a green carpet of ankle-high seedlings and it feels like a warm spring afternoon. There is that red wall again and I expect it is made from bricks even though it is still far away."

"I awoke from the deep sleep I was in and noted the time on the nightstand alarm clock – 3:16AM, at precisely the same time as the previous morning. Right after the dream I tried to concentrate on the details of the dream. It was the same field only this time it was green and grassy. Green! There was color in the dream and the sky was cloudless and blue! The wall was red, and I have a recollection of it being made from bricks although I do not remember any mortar, only an impression it was made from bricks. The day seemed warm but not hot. My brain ached to recall more but details would not come."

"That is just about it. What do you make of them?"

"Gee hon, I'm just not sure. Do you think they are something from your past? You know, kind of like you are reliving some event from long ago?"

"No, I'm quite sure I have never been in a field like that, and I don't have a clue about the wall. I suppose I should have just blown them off as a strange nightmare of sorts, but I am almost haunted by the feelings I had when I awoke."

"Oh, I am sorry, please try not to let it worry you." Rose consoled him, "Maybe you were just over-tired, and your mind was trying to find a place of rest. I am sure there is nothing to worry about. Seems to me your dreams of pastures are a peaceful place. Try to concentrate on that."

"Yeah, sure. By the way, you look particularly stunning this morning. Is there a special occasion?"

"Just the Quilting Guild at The Homestead Estate this afternoon. I am still searching for a new pattern to use for the next quilt I am making. A Christmas surprise for Jerry and Betty Hanson. They will never suspect!"

"Okay, I have a counseling session for the new couple at church at one o'clock. Jason and, what was her name? Hmm. Oh yes, Rose!" he joked at her name being the same as his wife. "They are going to get married later this year and they want to be sure they were meant for each-other. I will give them the 'leaving and cleaving' advise and hope it sinks in. Worked for us!

"I think I'll to go for a walk this morning and try to clear my head a little to sort things out. See you later after my appointment."

"That might be a good thing to do honey. Enjoy the walk." Rose said as Jon kissed her on the cheek and headed for the door. Rose was usually in an upbeat mood, always a smile and a hug but she was a little concerned about Jon and the effect of his dreams. "Hope he will put it to rest." She said to herself as she watched him disappear out the door.

3

Later Tuesday – Arlington Cemetery

Jon had a "usual" route he would walk when he tried to clear his mind over any topic, but today he headed out on the longer course that meanders through the Arlington National Cemetery. He always found a lot of solace in walking through the solitude of the rows of burial markers. Brings life's complexities down to a simple level, a humbling level, a respectful level. He cherished his walks through the historic grounds always leaving with a sense of purpose and a direction to take on whatever is turning over in his mind. He frequently passed through the John Kennedy Memorial on his walks and always read the inscription on the granite wall below the president's grave. Inspiring as it always is, Jon fixated on the last lines: "LET US GO FORTH TO LEAD THE LAND WE LOVE – ASKING HIS BLESSING AND HIS HELP – BUT KNOWING THAT HERE ON EARTH GOD'S WORK MUST TRULY BE OUR OWN." Jon turned that phrase over and over in his brain letting it deeply sink in.

"God's work truly is my own." He said aloud to no one, "I'm in this to help others, doing God's good works here on earth. I read somewhere once that old men will dream dreams and I guess I am sort of old, at least a little past mid-life. Maybe that is where the "dreams" part comes in, I am supposed to dream dreams. But what good are they if I cannot understand them?" No answer. Jon paused a few more minutes and re-read the granite inscription and said aloud the last couple of lines again hoping that some revelation might just strike him if he just read it one more time.

Leo, who was a groundkeeper at the cemetery for years, overheard Jon asking "nobody" his questions. Leo had a reason to be listening in since Leo was a Christian and his mission was to provide comfort to those who came to the cemetery mourning. You see, he not only worked there but he ministered there as well. "Hello stranger." Leo always said, as he greeted Jon. "I have seen you here before. Do you know someone who rests in his cemetery?"

"No one personally." replied Jon. "I come here to get away from life's troubles for the moment and try to spend some time in solitude and thought."

"I'll say Amen to that." Leo added but kept on "'God's Work Must Truly Be Our Own' is profound. My job is God's work. I care for this place; I care for people who visit here with a heavy heart. I offer them comfort as I explain my son rests here as well. As I care for my son, I will care for their child as well. It seems to help them cope. Usually, if they are OK with it, I will pray for them, and they almost never refuse. If they do refuse, I still pray for them. Leo is my name, and yours?"

"Jon. Hey, thank you so very much for the work that you do. Your story has touched my heart and I will always remember you. When I return, I will be looking for you."

"Jon, that is so kind of you, but please do not search for me. My mission here is for others and your mission is for your flock. The cemetery is large, and the workers are few. I must be going. Bless you, my friend."

"And you too as well." Jon replied as Leo turned to his work. John hustled off to meet with Jason and his soon-to-be bride. He was a couple of blocks away before he realized that he had not told Leo he was a pastor. How did he know?

~~~

"Hi Jason, Rose," Jon greeted the happy couple as they arrived at his office precisely at one. "Glad to see you are prompt for such an important meeting as we are about to have. Sit down and if you would like refreshments, I can get them before we start. Water? Soda? ... Nothing? OK, then, let us get started." Jon did his best to make the couple feel comfortable during this occasion of marriage counseling.

The three settled back into the comfortable leather chairs with the discussion directed by Jon and replies offered eagerly by the romantic couple. After prodding their degrees of commitment, extent of their belief and faith system, several "what if's" and "what would you do's" they called it quits after an hour and a half. One more session would be needed to cover the final topics, so a date was set for next week and off the starry-eyed two-some went to plan and plot other wedding details.

Jon made a mental note that these two did appear deeply in love and committed to the marriage sacrament and its meaning. "With the national average of half marriages ending in divorce I would guess they would be two of the fortunate ones to make it for life. I would give them a ninety percent chance in making it past twenty years." he proudly noted in their file. Jon was fully accurate in his prognostications, taking more credit than he deserved when he was right and was sadly disappointed when wrong. He was an optimist and always prayed his blessing on a couple would ensure a long life together, you know – 'til death us do part.

The rest of the day was entirely predictable, routine, and uneventful. Jon and Rose had their usual chit-chat over chicken-pot pies and spent the evening reading before retiring. Ho-hum. In the back of Jon's mind, he was wondering if he would have another dream tonight, hoping he would not but curious that he would.

4

Wednesday— Old Men Dream Dreams

The dream returned; the field was still covered in a knee-high carpet of wheat. At least that is what I would guess, it is probably wheat. Or maybe oats. I turned around and the field stretched to the horizon in every direction except straight ahead where the red wall was located. It was the same as the last dream except the wall somehow grew a little larger. The bright sun also warmed up the day.

There are two men standing quite a ways off to my left whom I hadn't noticed before, but they seem to be waiting and watching the field. Looking down I can see the soil of the field appears to be very dark and moist, the type of soil that would grow just about anything, extraordinarily rich.

~~~

He knew he had another dream and before his eyes opened, he remained motionless and tried to linger for a few moments and concentrate on the dream details. Jon looked at the clock, again 3:16

AM and he reiterated the dream in his mind, "The crop in the field had grown and had taken on the appearance of wheat or oats but that would be a guess. The wall seemed larger or was it closer? I am just not sure. Two men were there that I had not noticed before and they were just standing, pretty much the same as me. Lastly, the soil in the field was richer than any soil I had seen before, certainly a lot more fertile than the dirt in my part of the world." He had the same sense of dread or urgency he had felt the past two nights although still not sure why. The pattern of a more detailed dream each night for three straight nights was noted but any meaning or personal reason for the dreams was uncertain.

He made a mental note to investigate further in the morning but investigate where he did not have a clue. Fitfully he laid in bed until his brain settled down and he fell asleep again.

~~~

"Honey, are you going to sleep all day? I made you breakfast, and it will soon be cold." Rose called down the hallway to their bedroom.

Jon opened one eye and looked at the bedside clock. It Read 10:30. 10:30! "I never seep this late!"

"Are you OK?" Rose again called to him, but her concerns eroded as he came down the hall towards the kitchen pulling his bathrobe on.

"I never sleep this late! And you know what? I had another dream! This time, there were two men in the dream standing a ways off and they were just standing and waiting just like me. That is all they were doing, just standing. The wall grew bigger or else it was closer I could not really tell and the crop in the field was up to my knees. My impression it was wheat or oats. The day was brilliant and getting warmer. Same feelings of danger or urgency as well. That's all"

"That's still a bit strange. Three nights in a row you have the same dream." Rose said not knowing how to react but felt obligated to throw something out in response to the bizarre dreams.

"Not the same dream. Things change in subtle ways: the crop is taller, the day is warmer, the wall is larger, there are men in view that were not there before, but I still cannot figure out why this dream and why me?"

"I'm not sure what to say, Jon. Please give yourself some time, I am sure the answer will come to you. Eat your eggs before they get cold. It is a beautiful day outside and we are both heathy and have security in our lives. Why worry about a series of dreams? You have a lot to be thankful for."

Her reassurances did little to diminish his feelings and sense of urgency to do something. He felt he needed to act but could not guess what to do. "After breakfast I am going down to the church office and try to figure this out.

"What does your day look like?" he asked trying to change the subject.

"Nothing today, just some housework and shopping in the afternoon. Be gentle on yourself, you do not have to solve the problems of the world just because of some strange dream. Get an ice cream cone down at the dairy store and smell some roses."

Her optimism was just the jolt he needed to stop perseverating on his dreams. We would at least give it a rest until he sat down in his office to 'investigate.'

~~~

"Rose was right. I am letting this whole thing about dreams consume my every thought and action. I will stop at the DQ and get a chocolate dipped cone. Enjoy life, you only go around once I always say." The sweet treat did just the trick and kept his mind off his somber dreams long enough to get to the church, open the mail, and settle into his office

Once seated he wrestled with the thought of beginning his investigation by cleaning out one of his desk drawers, getting a cup of tea, checking the answering machine, and tossing some old papers. Finally, he could not avoid it any longer. He sat staring at a blank pad of legal paper. Hmm...

"Let's start with what I know and what I don't." Wheat, Oats, Barley, Other? A quick check of the internet revealed that his field was planted with a crop of wheat. The budding grains in the photos gave it away. "Wheat! I am standing in a wheat field. OK what else? Nothing."

As Jon was mulling the predicament of too many questions and not nearly enough answers, he heard a light knock on his door and as it opened a crack, he could just make out the silhouette of Bennie. Bennie or more formally Benjamin St. George is a homeless soul who befriended Jon on one of Jon's contemplative stroll around Arlington. Their personalities clicked and Jon spent the afternoon discovering the life of the homeless, Bennie's struggles with alcohol, his time in the service, a divorce, and a downward spiral toward hopelessness. In a sense, Jon was facing the same downward trajectory in his own life. He did not have a direction in life other than pastoring, his ministry had no real life, just existing, his flock were in a similar state without ambition to seek a deeper spiritual life – one hour a week was sufficient to appease their soul's yearning for connection. Jon and Bennie were commiserating buddies each drinking the wine of self-pity and loss of purpose.

"Hi Bennie! Come on in. Good to see you today. How are things?"

"Pretty much the same" Bennie answered as he found a familiar couch to rest his weary body. "Just came by to see if you had any chores I could do." This is a familiar dance the two went through to gain comfort in reestablishing their relationship. As usual, things settled down into a comfortable fellowship between the two. Jon caught up on the comings and goings of Bennie since they last met, laughing, and crying at the stories Bennie crafted from his recent trials. Eventually they got around to Jon, "What's going on with you? Rose still doing well?"

"Sure, she's still great, always keeping me out of trouble." They both chuckled. "Bennie, I've got to tell you about a series of dreams I have been having. I just cannot make much sense out of them and if they didn't have an emotional impact on me, I would have just blown them off as meaningless trivia." Jon went on the describe each of the three dreams he had over the past three nights recalling each aspect of the dream as best his memory would allow.

"Well, what do you think? Am I crazy or do you think there is something to this?"

"I certainly can't say, dreams never impacted me the way yours affect you. Maybe when I was a kid having nightmares or something but nothing significant. Surely the dreams recurring over three consecutive nights has got to mean something. The images you describe are not very revealing, and there does not appear to be a connection with the scene and your emotions. Anything more would be a guess. Sorry, Pastor."

Jon added "This whole thing of dreams seems to be consuming my every thought and I keep asking myself 'Why me, why am I dreaming this?'"

"Because you are an old man and old men dream dreams. Its scriptural you know." Bennie patiently explained.

"Scriptural? I didn't know that." Jon replied, a bit baffled. "I'll look it up. Thanks for stopping by Bennie. We both need to try to keep in touch more. I feel a special kinship in the times we share. Here, take this and get yourself a good dinner." Jon offered him a twenty. "You can get to those chores you mentioned some other time. Peace be with you."

Bennie politely refused the money but still accepted the gift as a down payment for future work. He thanked Jon and left the office just as discretely as he did his entrance. Jon sat there for a few moments pondering their conversation and replaying Bennie's dream response as scriptural. He reached for his Bible Concordance and looked up "dreams". There it was in Acts 2 verse 27 and he flipped to the verse in his Bible:

"In the last days, God says, I will pour out my spirit on all people. Your sons and daughters will prophesy, your young men will see visions, your old men will dream dreams."

"Well, I'm not that old." He told himself re-reading the verse. At this point Jon had to confront his spirituality, or rather the lack thereof. Jon somehow managed to comfortably develop a career in the ministry without any real sense of spirituality. That always seemed like a "Churchy" type of word, the type of word that satisfies the listener without really imparting any meaning. This assessment frightened Jon to his core and the thought of being a hypocrite as a pastor was more than he was willing to contemplate currently. Still, the seed was planted, he thought smiling at the connection to his dreams.

~~~

Over dinner Jon and Rose discussed their daily comings and goings and just as they were clearing the table Jon threw in an off-the-cuff statement: "Dreams are scriptural you know." He left out the part about 'old men'.

Rose nodded in agreement, and did not quite know how to respond, then added "I suppose they are."

The rest of the evening was quiet, and they both settled into their reading. Jon dozed off a couple of times before he finally decided to call it a day. Rose agreed and they headed off to bed in their usual routine except this time Jon put a pencil and paper on his nightstand, 'just in case' and turned out the light.

"Goodnight, dear."

"Goodnight honey."
"I love you."
"You too."

5

Thursday – Finding Faith

Well, here I am again. The field is certainly planted with wheat which is now obvious with the seeds beginning to bud on the stalks and the distant wall is distinctly larger because it is perceptually nearer though still at a distance –how close was impossible to tell without a sense of perspective of how tall the wall was. It was obviously miles away and it was incredibly large and ominous in its size and gravity. A sensation of movement rather than merely standing became obvious as wheat stalks moved past – now I am walking through the field! The air has a weight of summer-heat not formerly noticed and there was a breeze in the air now, coming from behind. The sky has lost its brilliant blue and was now a milky haze. The same two workers were still waiting out in the field, just beyond shouting range, their patience seemed natural as if they were waiting for a bus that would not arrive for some time. Last of all, I heard a tapping inside my head, though it was barely noticeable, the same as you would hear if you imagined someone rapping on a door. This detail would not typically make any type of impression except it was totally out of place in the middle of a wheat field.

~~~

3:16 AM was displayed on his alarm as Jon reached for his paper and pencil. The light was flipped on, and he began writing furiously capturing each morsel of memory he could scratch from this night's dream. The words and imagery filled up the entire page and he finished writing at the top of the second page. When he set the tablet down Jon was exhausted and depleted of emotional thought. The dream perplexed his consciousness and he ached for clarity and significance.

His head hit the pillow as he fell back into bed and a deep sleep washed over him like a blanket covering his head. These nightly visions were exhausting his soul.

~~~

Jon slept in later than usual for the second day in a row, extremely rare since he was not sick. Rose was already up and was fixing him breakfast when he finished his shower and got dressed.

"Good morning, Rose." Jon greeted his wife and gave her a soft kiss on her cheek. "It happened again last night. Same dream but more details. There were some slight changes from previous nights and this time I wrote down all that I could recall from the dream."

"What do you make of it?" she asked while flipping over his pancakes.

"I don't know. It's really got me stumped." After a pause, while Jon contemplating being stumped, "Maybe I will just have to wait to see what develops should I have more dreams."

"I hope you can get some answers and soon, dear. Sit down and we can eat breakfast together."

Jon ate pretty much in silence turning over his thoughts of those dreams. He ached for a clue, but it didn't come. Rose respected his thoughts and busied herself with cleaning up the kitchen. Jon finally concluded "It will have to wait; I need to pull together the sermon for Sunday. I will be at the office until two or so." His mind was still preoccupied as he got up from the table, gave Rose a hug and headed for the door.

"Don't be too late dear. Remember we have the Hanson's coming for dinner tonight. Maybe you and Jerry can try to figure this out."

"Thanks Rose. Gotta go. Love you"

"You too!" Rose was beginning to be concerned for Jon. As the door closed, she said to herself "This series of dreams is really starting to affect Jon. I hope he can find some peace about it soon."

~~~

Jon walked to his office at the church and was eager to get started on his sermon. The diversion from the dreams was a welcome change and he hoped it would clear his head.

Just like clockwork, Jon logged into his account at FreeSermonTopics.com and scrolled through their list of sure-fire sermon subjects. One that intrigued him was a sermon on dreams, so he double clicked on it and the whole sermon came up. He read through the prepared text, made a couple of changes to tailor it to his congregation, printed it out and was finished within the span of thirty-minutes.

Then he sat back in his chair. The hypocrisy of his life seemed so revolting to hm. Here he was a pastor of a large congregation, he was their shepherd, supposedly guiding them and inspiring them and he was a basket case. His trust and faith in God were shallow and his first thoughts of any challenging situation were always secular rather than spiritual. His rationale for his life was he was doing good works in his and Rose's life, he justified his job as pastor as "someone has to do it", and he had a degree from the diploma mill of "Divinity-U" who conferred on him a "qualification" and not a calling. He knew the routine from sermons to funerals and weddings, from counseling to conversations and he could talk the talk but had not a clue on walking the walk.

It had taken a homeless man to tell him that having dreams was scriptural and he had to look it up in a Bible to verify it. How sad. The bible, his source of thought-provoking verses wherein he could pull out-of-a-hat an inspiration when he needed one for a sermon, this Bible was confusing to him. He could not read it without becoming bored and critical as to its content.

"The crème de la crème was this series of dreams. It they are scriptural then what in blazes do they mean?" His helplessness to his situation caused him to pause and clear his thoughts. After a few moments he said out loud: "God, if you are trying to tell me something with these dreams you will have to help me understand!" Jon had never challenged God in this manner figuring God was always too busy to be concerned with what is going on in his little life. Then Jon waited.

When God did not speak to him, he thought "Maybe I should look in the Bible and try to find a scripture verse that might tell me something." So, he turned to the back of the Bible and found its small concordance and looked up "dreams" again.

He discovered the story of Pharaoh and Joseph when a line caught his eye: "Do not interpretations belong to God?"

"Interpretations! Interpretations! God, I am an old man dreaming dreams and I need an interpretation!" ... "Well? How can I hear you? How can you speak to me? What do these dreams mean?" Plenty of questions and answers were scarce. Jon felt like a blind man groping around in a strange city, hoping to bump into something familiar.

For the next hour or so Jon paged through his Bible, half reading, half skimming all the while expecting an epiphany to leap from the pages and everything would be clarified. The answers were just not coming, and he was growing more and more frustrated at his inability to gain insight as to his dreams. Finally, he gave up and decided to go for a walk.

The afternoon sun was warm with a slight breeze. The notorious DC humidity had not reached its suffocating levels yet, so the walk was invigorating. Jon was on his usual route where he did not have to pay much attention to his surroundings, like an old trail horse, his brain automatically knew the way home while Jon turned his thoughts over in his mind. His concentration was interrupted when a baseball rolled up and stopped in front of him. "Baseball?" he thought to himself.

"Sorry Mister!" a young boy apologized as he ran up to Jon.

Jon bent down and picked up the well-worn ball and tossed it back to the lad. "Here you go son."

"Thanks!"

"You're welcome and bless you." Jon replied as his automatic response kicked in.

"He always does!"

"He does?"

"Sure, Jesus blesses me all the time."

Well, that hit Jon squarely between his eyes. As he thought for a minute, "I cannot recall a single instance in my life where I was blessed, and I gave Jesus the credit for it." That thought hung in the air and Jon just could not make any sense of it. "Something in my life seems to be missing. It is like I am putting a puzzle together and I am missing a critical piece to finish it. I have all these loose ends in my life, and I cannot pull them together enough to understand what is going on." As he reflected on this he cried out "God, I need some help!" Again, no epiphany moment.

When Jon arrived home, Rose greeted him with a hug and asked how his day was. Jon shared some of his frustrations of the day and decided to just let them be since the Hanson's were coming for diner and Rose needed help with some of the finishing touches.

"Go wash your hands and give me a little help with these greens. We can discuss your day with Jerry and Betty later over some wine."

The rest of the preparations consumed the time until Jerry and Betty knocked on the door.

"Hi Jerry, Betty." Jon greeted them as he gave her a polite hug and shook Jerry's hand. "Come on in. Rose has a great dinner prepared for tonight and I am famished."

Betty replied, "It sure smells delicious, as always, whenever Rose makes dinner."

Jerry piped in, "What a talent, good looks and good cook too!" in a complimentary non-flirtatious way. "You are blessed Jon."

Jon thought a moment and then proudly agreed "Yes I have been blessed, and the Lord is still blessing me."

"Oh, for Pete's sake, come and sit down before the food gets cold." Rose said, deflecting from the compliments. "Are you guys hungry?"

~~~

Dinner was just chit-chat small talk until the delicious strawberry shortcake dessert was finished and everyone sat back in their chairs stuffed and satisfied. "Great dinner honey" Jon added, proud of his wife's banquet extravaganza. "I cannot eat another bite!"

"You out-did yourself on this one Rose!" Betty added.

Jerry concluded, "By far the best! Thank you so much!"

The table was cleared as the dishes were piled in the kitchen for cleaning in the morning. All four headed to the living room to relax and enjoy their favorite chardonnay. Jerry had been waiting for this opportunity, "Jon, have you had any more of your strange dreams this week?"

This was the lead in Jon needed and he opened with a full description of the dreams he had experienced to date. He ended with

"I am puzzled, confused and frustrated that they keep coming and I do not have a clue what to do about them. I have read in scripture that "Old men shall dream dreams", not that I am old mind you, and that God provides interpretations, again scriptural. But I have asked God what they mean, and I haven't even a single clue."

Rose added, "Those dreams seem to occupy a lot of your attention. I sure hope you can get some closure."

Jerry, who had been silent and deep in thought through Jon's listing of the dreams summarized, "So, please let me summarize what you just told us. You have a series of dreams that, from what you described, were remarkable and the impact you feel as being significant, perhaps even ominous. You can recall them in minute detail, unlike most dreams which fade quickly when you awaken. Your dreams pertain to situations and are full of elements not connected to any of your past experiences.

"The dream elements are a field of wheat, a huge wall, two workers, warm weather, and lastly a rapping sound. Progressing from the first dream you have noticed there is color in your dreams, you are moving about the field from a standing position initially, the temperature is getting warmer, the wheat is growing, and the wall is either getting larger or nearer. But the workers are not doing anything but waiting and in the last dream you remember hearing a faint rapping inside your head. Does that sum up what is going on?"

"Pretty much" Jon said.

"Aside from the dreams, you have told us that "old men dream dreams" even though you don't feel you are old." Everyone chuckled, "and dreams can have interpretations, which come from God. You say you have asked numerous people what they thought the dreams mean and have prayed for such an interpretation?"

"Correct." Added Jon, "That last part about old men and interpretations are from Scripture. I have prayed for the interpretation of the dreams but so far have not heard anything." He paused as they all contemplated Jon's last statement. "Oh, and one more thing, after each dream, when I awaken the time on my alarm clock has always been the same – 3:16 AM. That seems a little weird to me."

Jerry questioned, "Jon, 3:16 AM? Really?" The two couples just sat in deep reflection over Jerry's summation, trying to pull together any reasoning or thought to solve the mystery of the dreams. Finally, Betty softly said "When I was a girl, my Sunday School teacher would tell us that if God wants to tell us something, he certainly can but he has given us His word in the Bible through which he also communicates with us."

That thought hung in the air for a moment and Rose added "That's probably where you will find your answers, Jon."

"I tried that, I sat in my office for over an hour opening the Book and reading whatever verse my eye laid upon. It didn't say anything to me and only confused me and frustrated me." Jon declared, half with sarcasm and half with wishful hope. "I know a lot of proper verses that I can recite in the various circumstances I encounter as a pastor, but I cannot pull it all together."

Jerry tried comforting Jon, "You know a lot more about the Bible than I do Jon, but I think Betty is right. Your answers are probably in that book on your desk. You need to know how to find it and maybe another Pastor might point you in the right chapter to begin."

"Thanks Jerry, I think I'll take your advice and bounce this off another pastor in our council. I certainly hope he can help. Thanks for everyone listening and helping with your suggestions, they mean a lot to me, and all of your caring thoughts touch me more than I can say." Tears filled Jon's eyes as the enormity of their concerns and compassion flooded over his emotions.

From here the two couples broke out the canasta cards and wiled away the evening with trumps and melds. Finally, Jerry and Betty had to head home, and the evening came to an end.

As the front door closed and the house grew silent, Jon and Rose headed off to bed. Each was silently wondering if there would be another dream this night, as they prepared for bed and flipped of the lights.

Jon laid awake in silence for some time, turning over the evening's conversations. His mind ached to sleep but Jon fought it, partly in fear and partly in anticipation. Eventually, he drifted off.

6

Friday – Pastor Doug Kucher

The dream reappeared as vividly as before. Perhaps even more so as the scene surrounding me projected a higher dimension of detail, the individual stalks of wheat, now grown to waist high, remained visible trailing off into the distance as if Jon's vision improved greatly beyond a mere 20/20 level. The wall was moving closer, and the redness appeared more of a maroon, darker than before. The size of the wall was at least hundreds of feet tall rising majestically into the air. Its distance was still not discernable but nearer. The two workers were starting to prepare for their work, getting out supplies and they could be heard talking to each other though not loud enough to understand their conversation. They were wearing baggy clothing and wide brimmed hats to keep the sun off. Each wore heavy gloves and work boots. The sky was still hazy, but clouds were beginning to billow upwards toward the heavens and the wind freshened to a stiff breeze, again from behind. The stirring of the air brought with it dusty or perhaps musty odors typical of the rural setting. The heat was building, and a sweat started to drench my shirt. It's a bit bizarre, but I find myself saying these words aloud and I hear them as if spoken by a deeper voice. I start walking in the direction of the wall, again with the workers on my left, and discovered a railroad bed crossing the field with a few open-bin rail cars behind me. Strange that I had not noticed them before. I decide, although I am not sure why, to follow the rail path heading toward the wall. As I walk, I can hear my footsteps, my steady breathing, and this incessant knocking inside my head. I wish it would stop!

~~~

Jon awoke and realized immediately he had another of his bizarre dreams. He kept his eyes closed for a few moments as he filed away in his memory all the details. When he opened his eyes, he glanced at the clock and the digital display clicked over from 3:16 AM to 3:17 AM. "Man, this is creepy." thought Jon.

He sat up and turned the light on. With his pen and paper, he jotted down a few of his thoughts but he knew he would not forget any of the detail. One thing that struck him was the sense of sound this time that he had not noticed in earlier dreams. Whatever he could conclude from the dreams so far was that they were recurring, to the point of a culmination. What that may be was still a mystery, but he knew there would be more dreams.

He jotted a few final notes, shut off the light, and went back to sleep, confused but steadfast that the dreams would soon be resolved.

~~~

Jon's Friday morning routine for the past decade was to rise early and meet with the Friday Group down at the local coffee shop. He was the last to join the group that had been meeting for over twenty-five years, and as such, was always the butt of the "newbie" jokes. That was fine with Jon, he could take the ribbing as well as dish it out, but the reason he kept going each Friday was the fellowship and, at times, the wisdom he could impart through pastoral counseling.

The usual guys were in their usual chairs at the usual table when Jon entered the diner. Jon, as usual, sat in 'his' chair. After the typical banter of jokes and parodies and political posturing there was a lull in the conversation which Jon seized upon to get their feedback on his dreams.

"Seriously now, I have got to tell you guys about a series of dreams I have been having." Jon went on to tell of each dream and how they changed from one night to the other and how he had no clues as to their meaning or meanings. "I'm at a loss as to what to do. What do you guys think?"

Ron was the first one to jump in, "Have you tried not sleeping? No, seriously, it sounds to me like you have been given a message from God concerning something that is going on in your personal or professional life. No clue here what that may be though."

Lynn broke in, "There are several elements in your dreams that could be symbolic, such as 'clouds' might indicate a storm or stormy times ahead. Your problem is finding out what each symbol means."

Curt agreed with a nodding of his head. He was always a man of few words.

Finally, Lorin concurred with the others, "Sorry we couldn't help. Maybe next week, if you have more dreams, the answers will be clearer."

"Thanks for your comments, they mean a lot. I believe it is clear I need to find out what each of the symbolisms mean and then the overall answer will be clear." Jon got up and dropped a ten from his wallet on the table. 'I've got some research to do. Same time next week?"

All the other four agreed and each added a zinger just to remain in character while Jon headed for the door.

~~~

The morning was still cool, and the sun had not finished burning off the dew from the night before. "They were not much help." He thought as he headed down the sidewalk. He needed some fresh air to clear his mind. He replayed last night's dream again in his mind searching for significance and only found confusion and what is with that knocking sound? He meandered through a couple of streets being mindful of where he was and how to get back to his car. He was mostly focusing on the sidewalk bring sure not to trip over any changes in the cement surface when a sign caught his attention out of the corner of his eye – "Arlington Evangelical Church of Christ, Doug Kucher Pastor." Having caught his eye, it also caught his attention, He thought "Maybe I could talk to him about my confusion. I know I would be willing to help if someone came in off the street and asked me."

After a couple of knocks on the hefty oaken doors, the slightest waft of a man appeared, white hair in his eighties and wearing casual running clothes. He was obviously heading out for some exercise but paused a moment to help this poor soul at his door. "Can I help you?" he asked not sure if he really had the time.

"Yes!" implored Jon, "If you have a few minutes, I would be most grateful."

"Well come on in" said Doug waving his arm towards the sanctuary. "We can have a seat in the back row. My name is Doug, Doug Kucher, the head pastor here."

"I'm Jon Wyatt, pastor at First Presbyterian Church of Arlington." They sat down and waited for Jon to collect his thoughts.

"I don't know where to start." Jon blurted out as his brain was ready to do a data dump on the dear man.

"How about at the beginning." Doug offered with a gentle smile and encouraging demeanor.

"I have been having a series of dreams, not the ordinary ones about getting lost or falling off cliffs or hero sandwiches, but they follow each other from one night to the next, each building on the last by offering with more clarity and more confusion." Jon went on to explain each dream in as much detail as he could pull from his brain. "After each dream I have a foreboding sense of danger I cannot put my finger on what they mean, and here is the strange part, every night I wake up at 3:16AM! What does that say?"

"OK, let us break this down a little bit. You say Your name is Jon, right?"

"Yes."

"And the time is 3:16AM, right?"

"Yes."

"Jon and 3:16AM. Sounds like John 3:16, perhaps the most common scripture ever quoted from the Bible. *'For God so loved the world that he gave His only begotten Son, that whosoever believes in Him shall not perish but have everlasting life'*. My guess is that it is God who is trying to get your attention and the feeling you have is one of significance, whatever he is saying to you is significant."

"Yes, that's probably it all along."

"But I would guess, based on your confusion as to the content of the dreams and your description of a rapping or knocking sound in your head that you fail to see the biblical connections to what the dreams are about. You see dreams are scriptural in a sense that they are one way that God can talk to you without the chaos surrounding ordinary life during the day. That way the clarity of your dreams gets through creating a lasting impression that will stay with you in the upcoming day."

Jon added, "I have heard about old men dreaming dreams and the dreams have been clear as a bell and memorable."

"Precisely, now that knocking inside your head within the dream, is it possible that that sound is significant when you consider the scripture verse from Matthew 7:7 *"Ask and it will be given to you, seek and you will find, knock and the door will be opened to you."?* How does that fit in?

"Wow, there is a door in the wall, and the wall is coming towards the field that I am standing in. My only escape would be through that door! But I have to ask and seek?" Jon asked.

"You are looking for answers and I would guess the "Ask and it will be given to you" and "Seek and you shall find" pertain to your questions. You may have been asking and seeking but perhaps in the wrong place. The answers lie in the Bible where God's word can be found." Doug said.

"I believe I have known that for some time, but the Bible just does not speak to me, it seems so confusing and in an archaic language. Individual verses I can understand but putting them in context for me seem difficult to impossible." Jon said.

Doug encouraged Jon, "Of course it is, Jesus spoke in parable to confuse the Pharisees, but the common people understood the parable because they lived the parable and understood with their heart the parable's significance. I am going to ask you a direct question Jon, and I want you to be straight and honest with me. Jon have you been born again?"

Jon sheepishly answered "I'm not sure I am. Why would you ask that?"

Doug sat back and reflected a couple of moments. "Being born again is not the same as your mother giving you birth all over as impossible as that sounds. 'Born Again' means that your spirit is reborn and that you can understand what God is saying in his Word with your spirit, your soul, and not just your mind.

"It's simple and easy. Just repeat after me the following prayer and feel your words as if they are coming from your heart." Doug continued.

"Jesus, I believe you are the Son of the Living God." Jon repeated.

"And that I am sorry that I am a sinner in need of forgiveness." Jon repeated.

"Please forgive me of my sins, come in, and become Lord of my Life." Jon repeated.

Thank you and Amen." Jon again repeated.

"That's all you have to do. Jon, now you are born again. Your spirit has been released to guide you in the path of the Lord. You put off that decision for a long time didn't you Jon?'

"Yes, it was a long time. I guess I was just afraid and fearful about what that commitment would bring. And you know what? I sort of like it. There is nothing to be afraid of." Jon said with relief.

"Apply that spirit to the dilemma of your dreams and let the word of God direct your way. I have my opinion as to the meaning of your dreams, but you will have to find that out yourself."

"OK, Doug, I don't know how to thank you. Bless you for taking this time to meet with me. I am sure I will find my answers now." Jon said as he left Doug's church. It was amazing the calmness and yet giddiness he felt within his soul. It's as if he could now see life as reality when before it was confusion. He could not wait to get into his Bible back in the office.

~~~

The time between closing his car door in the church parking lot and his opening his Bible in the office was less than thirty seconds. Immediately he looked up John 3:16 and Matthew 7:7 and let both verses swirl around in his head, absorbing each within his soul. The words became a part of him, and the scope and depth of each verse magnified within his spirit. He re-read each chapter as the words were soaked up in his heart and with each verse his life took on new meaning. Joy filled his heart as he could now understand the significance of God's word. It had an immediate impact on Jon, particularly John 3:16 since it was now his verse, his name, his symbolic dream time and even his birthday, Jon was even born on March 16th. "What a coincidence!" he thought.

If that was all that God had for him in one day, then Jon's life would be overflowing but there were more blessings to come. He looked up 'harvest' he found Matthew 9:37-38 "*The harvest is plentiful, but the workers are few. Ask the Lord of the harvest, therefore, to send out workers into the harvest field.*" There were only two workers in the dream, I guess I should also be harvesting.

After pondering that he came upon Matthew 13:30 "*At that time I will tell the harvesters: First collect the weeds and tie them in bundles to be burned, then gather the wheat and bring it into my barn.*" WHEAT!! And Matthew 24:40 "*Two Men will be in the field, one will be taken and the other left.*" And verse 44: "*So you must be ready, because the Son of Man will come at an hour when you do not expect him.*"

Luke 3:17 spoke to Jon "*His winnowing fork is in his hand to clear his threshing floor and gather the wheat into the barn, but he will burn up the chaff with unquenching fire.*"

Jon sat in his chair memorized by what he had just read. The significance overwhelmed him. Jon, perhaps the least qualified of all pastors in the world, has been having revelations of the prophesized end times?

~~~

Rose was busy about doing her housework when Jon entered the Kitchen. He was later than usual, and it was starting to concern Rose. "Oh, I'm so glad you are home. I was starting to worry about you since you didn't call, and the hour was getting late. Are you all right dear?"

Jon didn't know quite what to say but offered "Yes, I am fine, but something happened today, and I need to think about it a little and share it with you after dinner."

Jon seemed detached from his home like his mind was miles and miles away. He left the kitchen to go sit in the living room in his usual chair, again focusing on nothing specific. Rose had never seen him in such a state and felt she should give him some space for now and expected to hear from him later.

Dinner came and went with each picking at their food. The news that Jon was carrying was running the gamut of all things tragic in Rose's mind. Cancer? Divorce? A death in the family? She couldn't fathom what was going on but held her tongue and gave Jon the time to assess what he was going to tell her.

As dishes were done, and things put away, the evening settled down to just the two of them in the living-room with a couple of lamps lighting a somber scene. Rose couldn't hold it anymore and quietly asked "Jon, what is it? I have never seen you like this in all the years I have known you. If its bad news, I can take it, but please just let me know."

Jon's eyes slowly raised from the carpet at which he was staring, and his eyes finally met Rose's. "After meeting with the guys at breakfast this morning I went for a walk going nowhere in particular just trying to sort things out and I suddenly stopped in front of the Arlington Evangelical Church of Christ. Something caused me to linger there. I knocked on the door and out walked the pastor, a guy named Doug Kucher. We chatted for a little bit, and he invited me inside where I told him about my dreams. He was more knowledgeable about the Bible, and he helped me with a couple things in my dreams."

"Jon, that's wonderful!' Rose joined in, "What did he say?"

"He drew a connection between my name and the time I saw on the clock after each dream. He put the two together and suggested it might mean John 3:16 – *"For God so loved the world that he gave his only begotten Son, that whosoever believes in him shall not perish but have everlasting life."* He connected that verse with the knocking in my head during the dream and gently asked me if I have given my life to Jesus by being born again. I told him no and he led me in the most powerful prayer I have ever prayed. And you know what? I have been born again!

"He sent me on my way, and I decided to go to the office and search the Bible to find other answers, but on the way, I was filled with such peace and joy such as I have never felt before.

"When I got to the office and opened the Bible, it was as if I had a new clarity and vision as to what the Bible was saying. I looked up scriptures and, though I had read them before, they now had a clear and vivid message specifically for me at this very moment, right now. The dreams I have been having are filled with imagery from scripture and I found verses that directly pertain to my dreams."

"Oh, Lord! Jon, this is what you have been hoping for! I am so happy for you. Can you pray for me to be born again too?"

"Sure, I can, its simple to do. Just repeat after me with all your faith and mean it from your heart." Jon then led her through the same prayer Doug led him through earlier in the afternoon. Jon just saved his first soul.

"Jon, I don't feel much different, but I do have a sense of peace after praying. Where do we go from here?"

"Well, I am not sure, but I have to find out if the verses that I discovered this afternoon point to the end of the world or if there is some other meaning."

"Challenge God to give you the answer." Rose immediately blurted out. "Where did that come from?" she wondered aloud at the immediate response.

"Wow, Rose, you are getting answers too. Let's pray that God reveals more about the dreams and what I need to do. I would be honored if you would speak a prayer."

Rose felt a new boldness as she opened her mouth and the words flowed out, "Dear Lord, we pray that you will give Jon answers to the dreams you have given him and the direction he needs to follow with your revelations. We thank you in the name of Jesus, Amen."

"That was perfect Rose. I'm sure I will hear something soon. He is faithful to answer prayers when we seek his wisdom." Where did that come from, he wondered, perhaps God is telling me he will provide answers!

They sat in the living room for several moments in silence, not sure what they should do. Finally, Jon said "God is in control, he will let us know when he is ready, in his timing. We will just have to be patient."

"You are right Jon. Let's get some of that strawberry shortcake I made yesterday, and we can talk about what has happened today."

The rest of the evening, Jon and Rose talked, laughed, and cried about the day and their lives together. Both were filled with a great joy and inner peace spending their first evening with born again spirits.

7

Saturday– A Sermon Rewritten

Jon lay in bed for hours constantly turning things over in his mind, trying to figure out for himself the meaning and significance of his life and his dreams. It was as if Jon were trying to see into the future and decipher what he should do to get there. It was futility at best. He kept going around in circles anticipating God's answers and then remembering he had to wait but maybe he wasn't doing his part to be more pro-active and search for answers, and on and on.

Jon was physically and mentally exhausted. He glanced at the alarm clock: 3:16 AM. He smiled and immediately drifted off to sleep.

~~~

Jon awoke with a jolt like he was being yanked upward into the sky. His sweat had soaked the sheets and his pajamas. His sweaty hair wet the pillow and he was getting a chill. He glanced at the clock 6:20 AM. The dream was seared into his brain's memory. He could recall with vivid intensity every moment and detail of the field of his dreams. He knew intuitively that he had received the answer to his prayers. The thoughts and imagery of his revelation humbled Jon and he started trembling at the thought that God would share this dream with him. Jon realized he must fully decipher the dream as soon as he could. He felt a sense of urgency he had never known before as he jumped from the bed.

Rose met him at the door having risen about an hour ago. One quick look at the soaked, disheveled man told her instantly "You have an answer, don't you?" The answer to her 'answer' was obvious. Jon looked at her nodding that she was correct and had a look of determination and urgency as he walked past her into the bathroom to get ready. "My man is on a mission!' she thought.

Jon showered and slipped into his weekend casual clothes. Thought after thought raced through his brain creating a never-ending list of to-dos for the day. Rose had his egg and toast ready when Jon entered the kitchen and after a quick prayer of thanks, he devoured the meal and told his wife "I've got to go now, I have a sermon to write for tomorrow and the ideas are flowing. I will be back home from the church as soon as I can. I love you!" With that said, Jon was out the door, into his car and headed straight for his office.

Once at his desk he sat at his computer and was ready to type. His old sermon he had downloaded for tomorrow was thrown into the wastebasket like yesterday's newspaper. That sermon just would not do and the thought of using it made him queasy. "How could I have ever given such garbage to my congregation before?" he wondered out-loud to himself.

For the next couple of hours Jon sat at his desk composing the first real sermon of his life. While feeling ashamed that it came so late in his life, he also was proud that he had a motivation to express the revelation given to him from God. With the first draft completed Jon read and re-read the sermon making changes, correcting spelling and grammar, adding emphasis here and deleting extraneous thoughts there.

When it was done, Jon sat back in his chair and looked at the neat stack of paper on his desk. There it was, a masterpiece given to him from God, as a message to His people. Jon was humbled and felt so unworthy to be the bearer of such a gift.

There was an unexpected knock on the door and Jon went to answer it. Outside was a pleasant young man who asked if he could spare a few minutes. Jon agreed and they went to his office.

"My name is Charles. Charles Randall but you can call me Charlie. You might have read some of my commentaries in the papers over the last few years." Jon indicated he had not, but Charlie continued, "My father is a good friend of Pastor Kucher who I believe you met yesterday. I guess Pastor Kucher wants me to interview you about a series of dreams you had. Could you spare a little time to help me out? I can't promise it will get published but the topic intrigued me, and I want to explore this further."

Jon felt honored that someone else other than his friends and family was interested in his dreams, so he willingly gave Charlie his interview so as not to miss any detail Charlie also taped their conversation. Charlie thanked Jon when they were through and quietly let himself out the door.

As Jon was contemplating his previous visitor, the phone rang, and it was Rose.

"Hi, darling." Said Jon.

"Honey, are you alright? You have been gone for so long and we need to be planning supper. Will you be much longer?" Rose asked.

"I'm great! I just finished my first original sermon." Jon boasted and then sheepishly added "I am embarrassed to say that it should have been written decades ago."

"Now, Jon! You know that God does not call the qualified, he qualifies the called. You were meant to write that sermon, it is your thoughts and emotions given to you by God, and now you are the willing vessel to deliver God's message."

"You're right. I will be home in ten minutes, see you then sweetie."

~~~

After diner, Jon sat Rose down and read through the entire sermon. She was blown away that Jon could write such a masterpiece and was so excited that she had to call Betty. "You have to go to church tomorrow Betty and be sure Jerry comes too. Jon's got his answer to the strange dreams he has been having and you just need to hear it. Be sure to be there!" Rose was so excited she hung up before giving Betty a chance to say anything.

The phone almost immediately rang, and it was Betty calling back with a slew of questions, most were answered with a "You will have to wait and see." – or – "I know!" their conversation drifted into the background as Jon went into the bedroom to re-read his sermon again.

At ten o'clock they settled into bed and chatted nervously about the morning service and how the sermon's impact would affect the congregation. Happy in their thoughts they both drifted off into a restful sleep.

PART TWO: THE HARVEST

8

Sunday – Dreams of Peace

"Floating. The word choice was a poor one since it only described about a tenth of what I am feeling. Floating, with no weight or a sense of "up" or origination or destination. Just floating. Any stress that was once in my body has long since dissipated. Muscles have yielded and relaxed. My eyes naturally close but also naturally open without expectation of seeing. There was light but it was coming from all directions much like when you fly through a cloud. I noticed nothing familiar with my sense of smell although there is a flowery aroma wafting from nowhere. I felt warmth but not heat as the temperature was ideally perfect. No wind and I felt absolute comfort relaxing in and being in this floating. Serenity, peace, no worry as time just vanishes away. Aaahhh!"

~~~

Hmm... Huh? ... Oh, let me stay. Sleep began to escape Jon as the morning beckoned his brain to start dealing with the day. Slowly his eyes parted and in front of him was the alarm clock proudly beaming 6:20 AM. "Oh, I have to get up and get going." Jon muttered to himself as the blankets were swept aside and he sat up on the side of the bed, cobwebs clearing from his brain. The sermon... Oh THE SRMON he thought as a shot of adrenalin coursed through his veins. I have got to get going.

Rose was still asleep, so Jon quietly got up, put on a pot of coffee, and jumped into the shower. The hot water soothed his still-tired muscles as he slowly laid out his day. Dressed and leaving the house at 8:30, open the church, review the sermon one last time. Same old routine except today will be different. His congregation is surely in for a surprise, just hope they will receive what I have to say.

With breakfast consumed and the pair each going through their usual Sunday morning routine, spent mostly in silence, they soon found themselves in the car driving to church. Rose opened the conversation sensing the tension that was building in Jon "Do you feel OK to be doing this today?" she gently asked.

Unpredictably, Jon softly answered with a sense of regret, "I should have been doing this for decades. I just pray the members will receive my sermon in the spirit I will give it. There are so many in our church that need to hear what I have to say." He looked at Rose for confirmation.

She proudly smiled at Jon, looking him in the eyes, she said, "You are at this point in time for a reason. It doesn't matter what happened last week or last year. What IS important is today and what you are going to do with it. I believe the anointing is upon you, you just have to step into it and God will respond."

Jon drove again in silence, turning over in his brain Rose's response. As they were turning into the church parking lot he finally said, "You are right, as usual. I am but a single man and can only to what I can do. The rest is up to God."

Jon went into his office to review his sermon. Rose went into the sanctuary to be sure all the preparations were in place for the service. Little did Rose think about her conversation with Betty last night, but she did mention to Betty the events of the day that happened to Jon and how excited she was at the re-birth of Jon's enthusiasm for the Gospel. It appears that Betty spent the evening contacting the prayer team who then canvassed the entire congregation to be sure to attend the morning service. The response was overwhelming as the spirit moved the members to attend in force!

Extra seating was added in the front and back of the pews as the over-flow was asked to stand around the back of the church. A sense of expectation was in the air as the service was set to begin.

Jon came into the sanctuary from his usual entry behind the pulpit and was astonished to see a standing room only crowd crammed into his church. He took his seat as the opening song was started. The volume and intensity of the singing aroused the spirit in Jon fostering a sense of calm and purpose and confidence.

As Jon sat reflecting on his mission, he recalled arising the last two days at 6:20 AM. 6:20, what does John 6:20 say? He hurriedly thumbed through his bible hastily arriving at John Chapter 6, verse 20 which reads: *But Jesus said to them, "It is I, do not be afraid."*

After the announcements and offering it was time.

9

The Sermon

I stood to my feet, knees wobbly and unsteady. My mouth was dry, and a roar was deafening in my ears though I am sure no one else had heard a sound. I looked out into the congregation, into the faces of the gathered, my heart discerned their souls, some saved and many not, and my heart was filled with an overwhelming love for everyone staring back at me. God had groomed me for this moment, for this time, for this opportunity to reap his harvest. My sense of purpose and confidence escaped me at the thought of God's reliance upon me. I staggered toward the podium and surprised myself that I transcended the several feet without falling miserably. For what seemed like an hour, though actually only a few seconds I stood frozen. Panic overcame me as this unworthy vessel seemed to lack the capacity to pour out His message. I struggled to assess my opening thought as I opened my mouth to speak terrified that I would, not – could not. Then I remembered – 6:20 "It is I, do not be afraid." It was at this moment, this instance of faith, that the Holy Spirit entered the sanctuary and washed over me. His strength became my strength, His boldness became my boldness and I said:

"I stand before you a humble man. I am a simple pastor, your pastor, living out a simple life and comfortably I was heading toward retirement although when I was not certain. That is until I went to sleep last Sunday evening. You see, this past week has been a week like no other in my entire life.

"Sunday night, actually in the early hours of Monday morning I had quite a simple dream. In my dream I was standing in a field that stretched to the horizon in all directions, it was daytime, and there, in the far distance I could discern something like a wall, so long it disappeared into the horizon. It was 3:16 in the morning when I awoke, groggy yet wide awake at what I felt was a significant dream. I was confused as I tried to attach meaning to the odd dream that, for some reason, evoked importance in my mind.

"Then that night, early on Tuesday morning, I awoke after again having the same dream but there were a few small differences. This time the dream was in color, a green carpet of plants covered the field, the sky was blue, it was a warm day, and the wall in the distance was a brownish red the color like bricks and it was slightly bigger. I woke up and made a mental note to remember the details and, curiously, was surprised to see the clock displayed the same time as the previous night's dream.

"If you see a pattern here don't be surprised, I noted it too. The next night, again early on Wednesday morning, same time, same bed, I had the same dream again but with some changes. Now the plants were knee high, and I had the impression that the crop was wheat, although I am not a farmer, so I don't know where I came up with that idea. The wall again seemed closer, the day was warmer than before, and I noticed there were two workers off to my side at a distance. They were too far to hear what they were saying but thy were just standing there, watching the field. The field also had, what I thought, was the richest soil I had ever seen, again, not sure what that meant. When I awoke those details were seared into my brain and again the same curiosity of waking at 3:16 AM.

"The next night, early Thursday, - same time, same place, same dream, but with more changes. The plants definitely were wheat as the kernels were now developing, the day seemed like midsummer with its stifling heat, I noticed the wheat moving past me as I was walking forward, towards the wall. The two men at my side were still patiently waiting, like you would for a bus, the wall was obviously bigger and nearer although I was not sure how tall it was. The sky lost its deep blue and now was a milky haze from the thickening humidity of the mid-afternoon and I heard a distinct knocking coming from somewhere, perhaps within my head. Again 3:16 AM

"For those who are keeping track, that's four nights in a row, all at the same time and about the same dream but with more details each night. I have had two more dreams, but I will get to them.

"Later in the day on Thursday a particular verse was revealed to me – its Acts 2:27 which says *"In the last days, God says, I will pour out my spirit on all people. Your sons and daughters will prophesy, your young men will see visions, your old men will dream dreams."* I somewhat resent being referred to as old, but I suppose I am elderly and that's close enough. From this verse I can conclude that God is giving me these dreams

"Thursday night, early Friday morning, the dream recurred: my vision improved beyond 20-20 with fine details evident everywhere I look. The wall was moving toward me and was hundreds of feet tall. The two workers were preparing to labor putting on work clothes, hats, and gloves. The sky was hazy, and a stiff wind blew from behind. Heat was building and the air was dusty and musty from the rural setting when I came upon a railroad bed that I followed toward the approaching wall. All the while that same knocking was going on in my head. Again 3:16 AM.

"Friday, the day before my last two dreams, my life totally changed. I became born-again through the guidance and counsel of Pastor Doug Kucher at Arlington Evangelical Church of Christ. He explained the knocking sound I heard the previous night was Jesus standing at the door and knocking as described in Matthew 7:7 *"Ask and it will be given to you, seek and you will find, knock and the door will be opened to you."* I needed that door to be opened to me so I could understand what was going on. Doug then drew a comparison between my name and the time of my dreams – Jon and 3:16AM to the most popular verse from the bible -John 3:16 *"For God so loved the world that he gave His only begotten Son that whosoever believes in him shall not perish but have everlasting life".* Everlasting life! Pastor Kucher led me in a simple prayer that birthed God's spirit in me – it was born anew, and I was reborn. I was saved. I was granted salvation. With the Holy Spirit in my heart, I was able to read scripture and interpret it with my heart as well as my brain. The scriptures became real to me, I shared this with Rose, and she too was saved. We both rejoiced and shared this blessing into the late night. As I fell asleep my last conscious thought was to glance at the clock and was not the least surprised to read 3:16AM, Saturday morning.

"As my head hit the pillow I quickly fell into a deep sleep and began to dream. To capture the significance of that dream I would like to read from my notes written down when I awoke:

"I realize I am in the dream again but there is chaos everywhere. The wind is howling from behind me with a wail I have never heard before and it smells of burning weeds that sting my nostrils. Ash is flying past me with bits of harvested wheat stalks as if blown by a tornado. The

two workers were furiously swinging their sickles carving great swaths in the ripened wheat. The severed stalks laden with kernels flew into the air and were separated by the wind into stalks and kernels. Unexpectedly, the stalks settled to the ground and were instantly consumed by fire while the kernels were blown upward, high into the air and out of sight. This harvesting was an instantaneous and endless process performed by the workers laboring, in their furor, to gather the entire harvest. I thought to myself: "Why are there not more workers?

"The sky was billowing with storm clouds growing darker by the second as if to unload their torrent upon the furious activity in the field. The rail cars, filled with grain from previous harvests were rolling on the tracks, gathering speed, careening toward a small door in the wall. The wall. THE WALL! The wall, that a day earlier appeared so far so away was now nearly upon the field. It reached higher in the air than the approaching storm clouds. Nothing could go over it or around it. Its momentum would not be stopped as it moved towards the field in front of me and the storms fury approached from the rear creating a cataclysm of opposing irresistible forces. Torrents of rain, hail and lightning ripped loose from the sky immediately soaking me, the workers, and the field. My thoughts were in conflict; self-preservation in the face of such adversity or throw myself into a final frenzy of harvesting. Out of nowhere, one of the workers disappeared. I raced to join in the harvest grabbing his sickle and began to cut giant swaths in the ripened wheat. The incessant downpour and the approaching wall were inconsequential in my desire to swing the sickle one more time, one more time. TIME! That wall represents time! Insatiably moving forward, never ceasing, stopping, or waiting. The wall of time approaching, marching to the beat of a second-long metronome. Closer, closer, closer every second the wall trampled the field directly in its path. It was the last race against time I was waging as the wall was gaining on me. I turned away from it and concentrated on the harvest. My back ached and my arms screamed for rest - one more swing, one more time. The wall was almost upon me when it slowed to a crawl allowing me to harvest ever more wheat. One more swing, one more time, one more swing, one more swing, one more swing, one mo...

"I sat up! The time was 6:20AM."

(After a long pause to let the congregation absorb the dream) "God, for whatever reason decided to choose me to receive these dreams, these visions. I have, in humility, passed them on to you. Now you must decide what God is saying to you through me. Let me give you something to consider.

"The wall. That ever-approaching wall represents time. Not just time in general but finality of time. End time. Whether as an individual end of life or collectively for humanity at the end of the ages. The time marches forward without stopping and God knows that moment in time for each of us. God knows your individual time and he knows the time of the great harvest of souls. See Matthew 24:36 *"About that day or hour no one knows ... but only the father"* or Acts 1:7 *"It is not for you to know the times or dates the Father has set by his own authority."*

Consider also, the environment of the dreams spanning an entire growing season. This gives you a clue that we can discern the season of God's harvest by paying attention to what is happening around us. Consider the weather, in God's wrath he will *"unleash a violent wind, in my anger, hailstones and torrents of rain will fall with destructive fury."* Ezekiel 13:13: Consider the workers bringing in the harvest, two initially then only one. *"The harvest is plentiful, but the workers are few."* Matthew 9:37 and *"Two men will be in the field; one will be taken and the other left."* Matthew 24:40.

Finally consider the wheat. These are the souls of mankind ripened and ready for the harvest. The wheat has chaff and kernels represented in the harvest by the wheat kernels arising upward into heaven, "taken" so to speak and the chaff falling to the ground burning as in Matthew 3:12 *"His winnowing fork is in his hand, and he will clear his threshing floor, gathering wheat into his barn, and burning up the chaff with unquenchable fire."*

So, in summary, we will have a great harvest of souls, the season is ripe for the harvest as we can see in the season of our society being ripe for the harvest; We have harvest workers to bring home the souls and we have time marching to the beat of a metronome, incessantly growing closer minute by minute to an exact moment of time we do not know except only that it is coming.

Time marches on one second at a time, as soon as a 'second' arrives it is gone. What we do with our multitude of 'seconds' constitutes our life. Within those uncounted groups of seconds comes frequent opportunities to call upon Jesus to be our Lord and Savior. Our acknowledgement and submitting to that awareness determines if we become wheat by accepting Jesus or if we become chaff by denying Jesus, it is an "either – or" decision. Either you freely accept the gift Jesus is offering for salvation or you reject his offer, nothing in between.

I will now give you an opportunity to accept the gift of salvation, offered freely by Jesus. It may not be your last opportunity or just maybe it will be the last. If you do accept this gift, your destiny is sealed, your place in the harvest secured when the wall of time is finally at hand. For those of you who reject this gift, for whatever unjustifiable reason, the wall still approaches. It may be here in five minutes, five days, or fifty years. No one knows. but I assure you, without embracing the gift of salvation, your indecision will become a decision and chaff you will be, and just as certainly the chaff will burn.

The decision is yours, accept or reject. But if you choose to accept, I offer John 6:20 *"Jesus said to them. 'It is I, do not be afraid.'* "

I invite all who wish to freely accept the gift of salvation, paid for by Jesus Christ's death on the cross for our sins to repeat after me." which Jon repeated exactly as Doug Kucher had led Jon.

At the conclusion of the prayer Jon assured the newly saved souls, "in the words of the old hymn, Amazing Grace – 'I once was blind but now I see' because 'I was lost but now I'm found.' Thank you for hearing my testimony. Peace be with you; may the Lord shine his face upon you and be gracious unto you. God bless you."

Hundreds of souls were added to the wheat column, snatched from the chaff column. Shouts of "Hallelujah" and "praise the Lord" were proclaimed everywhere as Glory was re-established in Arlington First Presbyterian Church for the first time in decades.

Amid the celebrations, one person stood at the back of the church. He smiled a knowing smile and Doug Kutcher quietly slipped out of the church.

10

Monday – Viral Sermon / The Team

The dream of floating had returned just as satisfying and peaceful as the previous night but with a twist. Round about my floating body appeared a ribbon of color*, white at first, then it changed to bright blue, then to a deep red, then to brilliant yellow, earthly green, and on and on through all the colors of the rainbow. Then it repeated the process at a quicker tempo. Then again at a slower rate. It was mesmerizingly beautiful as it completely enveloped my attention.

When I awoke, I noted the time. Again, it was 6:20. Jon smiled, jotted down some comments, and drifted off to sleep again.

~~~

After Charlie's interview with Jon on Saturday, Charlie knew he couldn't miss the sermon on Sunday. In fact, for some reason, Charlie brought along Tim, his cameraman and Larry his sound guy, to record the sermon. The subsequent tape was shown to his publisher early on Monday morning but not before Charlie read him the notes on the backstory to Jon's sermon. Charlie's publisher seemed to be satisfied and made a strange remark about Doug Kucher. I asked him to clarify his comment and he acted as if I was prying a secret from him that he was not supposed to reveal. Since the beans were already spilled all over his desk, he finally admitted that Doug Kucher wanted to see Charlie right after their meeting.

Now, as moving, and impressive as Jon's story was, Charlie had full intentions to move on with his next assignment and now was being drawn back into Jon's story and the mysterious Doug Kucher, family friend but unknown to Charlie. "Very well, I will go see this Doug Kucher and find out what he has to say." Charlie said defiantly, irritated that he was being dragged further into the ministry of Jon Wyatt.

~~~

Jon had recalled the day before when his life was turned upside down and his first "sermon." Members of his church, and just about all the extra brethren who could make it to First Presbyterian on Sunday were calling his home throughout the day on Sunday and even a few more this morning were thanking him for such a spectacular message he had delivered. There were a couple naysayers who threatened to resign from the church membership, but they were overwhelmed by joyous members and visitors celebrating Jon's greatest-ever first sermon.

His daydream ended when he got THE call, the one he was anticipating most, the person to whom he could express his heart-felt gratitude and appreciation. Rose answered the phone and without saying a word, turned to look at Jon with a grin as wide as her heart, she held out her arm to hand him the phone.

"Jon, Jon? You there?"

"Uh, yes. Yes, I am Pastor Kucher." said Jon, stumbling over his words.

"Just call me Doug, son. I need to speak with you. I have a meeting that I have arranged and would like for you to see me at my church this morning at eleven. Can you make it?"

"Um sure." Jon said.

"Oh, by the way. You made an old pastor immensely proud yesterday. See you at eleven and bring your lovely wife with you."

~ ~ ~

Jon and Rose both arrived a couple of minutes early and the church secretary escorted them to the pastor's chamber where Doug was waiting. Shortly, Charlie Randall arrived and was shown the way to the pastor's office where everyone exchanged pleasantries and were introduced to a Mr. Arnold Sullivan. "Arnie", as he like to be called, was the Station Manager of the local affiliate of a major news network. Charlie had run into Arnie in his earlier travels in DC and Charlie believed he was recognized as well.

With the small talk completed we all settled into comfortable chairs. All eyes expectantly looked at Pastor Doug who then took the queue to begin.

"Well, I wish to thank you all for coming this morning on such short notice but as you will soon see, time is of the essence *"The Harvest is great, but the workers are few"*. I believe you used that scripture in your sermon yesterday, correct Pastor Wyatt?"

"You are right Doug. I did notice you slipping out of my church right after the sermon. I had hoped to greet you in person."

"I had lots to do, and I hope you understand. And you Mr. Randall, I am glad to finally meet you. Your dad has a lot of great things to say about you. So, it was at his recommendation that I reached you through your office to meet with Pastor Wyatt last Saturday, to get to know him and his remarkable story." Doug explained.

"I want you all to know that when Jon wandered into my church last Friday, he was a downtrodden, confused man. After our short conversation he was greatly encouraged and had a determined attitude when he left, and it was then that I put out a request to your dad to forestall your next assignment and squeeze Jon into your schedule.

"I saw something special in Jon's demeanor before and after our short visit. Whenever I have seen that look, in the three or four times of my life, I knew something big was going to happen. And indeed, it did."

"I was so pleased that you too saw something special in Jon to attend his sermon, care to expand upon on that?" Doug asked, pointedly to Charlie.

"Um, I can tell you this. I was greatly surprised to interview Jon. My writing specialty is more along the line of criminal activities but the personality and charisma that Jon effused drew me in and I just had to see how his sermon would be received." And he proudly added, "Perhaps it was a nose for news that I have but I could not resist the urge to line up a film crew for the next morning. Whatever was going to happen I knew it must be documented on video."

"Indeed, you did." Doug said, "And I saw you directing the crew to blend into the church so as not to disturb the movement of the occasion. I am proud you performed in a professional manner, anticipating something BIG was about to occur. Knowing you were there, gave me the peace of mind to put away my smart phone. I would simply rely on your tape.

Then turning again to Jon, he said "More than the few hundred people at your church need to hear your words, feel your humility, and be thrilled by your passion! We are going to go BIG!

"This leads me to Artie." Doug said looking in Artie's direction. "Artie has been a deacon at our church for over twenty years. His counsel and faith are greatly valued by this church. When I described the past, few day's events with Artie this morning, his confirming reaction was to go BIG, his words not mine. Before he could say anything more, we paused and said a prayer in agreement to be led by God in His definition of BIG. Artie then submitted to me what he felt God meant by Big and his definition was mine as well – the world. This must be shared with the world. Not in a passive, "put the word out" and pray that it grows, inspires, and spreads. Tell us what your plan is Artie."

Artie replied, "I just finished speaking to my staff and had a conference call with the national network. They all agreed if BIG is the world, then we need to form a team of broadcast experts, producers, engineers, outreach ministries, advertising, and promotions, print and video to promote interest, satellite engineers to up link and distribute the signals across the globe. National and international broadcast networks to coordinate signals to countries without satellite links, the list goes on and on and on. Normally this type of effort would take anywhere from six to twelve months to get proper clearances, permits and approvals."

Doug jumped back in, "I want this to happen next Sunday. If we start today, if we align efforts and world leaders grant permissions to bend rules, we could possibly get it done in one month. If God is in it, one week will be sufficient." Arnie had an exasperated hopeful look on his face and the group slowly turned to Jon.

"Why would God not be in it?" Jon rhetorically asked. "I will go where I need to go, stand where I need to stand, say what I need to say. I will swing the scythe to continue the harvest, and swing it again, and again, and again. Until the harvest is complete, or I expire."

Jon could not believe he just said that. The rest of the room just sat there stunned and everyone knew Jon was right. Finally, after an exceedingly long three second pause, Doug said "Then let's do this. The next group we need to get involved is the prayer warriors, the intercessors – they will lay the groundwork for all else to rest upon, they will open doors, remove spiritual impediments, draw resources where none exist, expect miracles and so on. They at best will march right behind the direction that God leads them. Artie, I want you to get this going. Meet me back here at three this afternoon.

"Mr. Randall, I need you to get that tape and your report down to Artie's station where the film will go out on the internet in its entirety. This must be done so that skeptics can go somewhere and be convinced this needs to happen. Your report will be sent to a team of translators who will distribute it worldwide over the next couple of days. When you are done, please get in touch with Artie. He should have further directions for you."

"Rose, I need you to keep Jon grounded. Keep the same routine you typically follow. Be sure Jon eats and is well rested. Don't let him overthink what he needs to do. The week will pass quickly.

"Jon, I need you to pray that God gives you revelation as to any fine tuning of your message. Go online and download your sermon and review it and make changes, if and as needed when God directs. Do not overthink what needs to be done. Listen to your heart, it will tell you if you are going in the right direction or not. If you do not find peace, then make no changes.

"You all have your assignments. Please give me time to do mine and I will be back in touch soon."

Doug's next call was to the church intercessors headed by Sophia, brought her up to date as to the morning meeting. "I know I called you Saturday about something big that might occur this week. Well, I now know this is God, and it's going to happen.

"Please call your team together early this afternoon, absolutely important and highest priority. In addition to their prayers, you will need to bring in the next level of intercessors, get them to watch the video coming out in the next couple of hours of Jon Wyatt's Sermon, tell them to search for that. Ask each of the next level of intercessors to pass this along as quickly as you can to further contacts, getting this as far out as you can. Include missionaries and their teams as well. Set up communication lines and links, back and forth, so updates can be distributed, and obstacles can be removed quickly. Remember that we will be opposed spiritually, and we will overcome any roadblocks. Any questions?"

Now Sophia was a take charge type of person and was two to three steps ahead of Doug as he was explaining. Sophia knew the power of prayer. She also could tell from Doug's demeanor that this was going to be memorable, and her role was paramount to it being successful. Sophia's response to Doug was short and sweet – "I won't let you down and I won't let Jesus down."

Doug nodded and smiled a knowing smile. "Check that one off my list!"

11

Tuesday – WW Vision / Time Crunch

The dream began the same as Sunday morning but changed again to the ribbon of my dream on Monday but then took on a whole new dimension with multiple ribbons twirling about my body flashing more colors than could ever be conceived. The ribbons would separate and then weave in and out forming a kaleidoscope of color impossible to imagine. The weaves and spinning of the ribbons vacillated in speed, rhythm, motion, and texture. It was such an entertaining and giddy spectacle I wished it to never end.

6:20 AM. Notes jotted down. Knowing smiles and a return to restful sleep.

~~~

Charlie called Pastor Kucher first thing this morning to report his progress in uploading the video of last Sunday's sermon. It was loaded by 1 PM and was already going viral with over twenty thousand views worldwide and I must admit this vastly exceeded my expectations. When he reported the number to Doug, he kind of shrugged it off, "it will do better by the end of today."

"I thought it was quite remarkable. Videos of this nature take a while to get the word out before taking off." Charlie said waiting for him to acknowledge the achievement.

"Charlie Randall, with the power of the Holy Spirit working in our midst a hundred thousand views is not very much, but His timing is what's important. Let me fill you in on what has happened in the last 24 hours.

"Artie has advised that a date has been set for our world-wide outreach, it is this Friday at Noon our time. Too many countries just couldn't make it happen on Sunday, the logistics just wouldn't work. Saturday was out as well with the Jewish Sabbath, so we are left with Friday, early so that Europe would be able to be available to watch without being too late. Noon on Friday is our target.

"Jon is doing well. He slept well last night and is praying about any tweaks he needs to make to his sermon. I heard from the President last night, he called me to offer any support we need from his administration. He gave me several contacts to call to get things rolling.

Doug paused for a moment, tapping his pencil on the table. His eyes stared deeply into Charlie's soul, and he said, "Mr. Randall, are you going to continue on with us, at least through the rest of the week? I have got a lot of things for you to do if you are willing."

Charlie's first impulse was to make up something, anything, to get out of this mass of confusion and on with his next assignment but he found himself nodding and saying "Sure, what do you want me to do?" *I have no idea where that came from, something inside me just blurted it out and what's even stranger – I can't wait to get going.*

"Artie will put you into contact with someone he works with to get social media up and running with this. Not only in the US but worldwide. You'll probably need to edit down the video you have to the salient points and get some script from Artie for content – he may need your expertise with the wording too. Give him a call as soon as you can. We need to get this up and running today."

"I'm on top of it. I will reach out to Artie as soon as I am out the door." Charlie replied.

"Great! Oh, one more thing, keep me updated with texts as to the viewership of the sermon." Doug quickly added "And thanks, your help has already opened many doors and will continue to do so."

Doug's next attention was to call Sophia. He brought her up to date about what had occurred during the morning. Sophia's reaction was of solemnity and praise – "God's in it. He is going to do this." She then added – "I have the team up and praying about the communications details coming together perfectly and social media reaching uncounted millions of souls in the next two days."

"Thank you, Sophia, I knew I could count on you."

Doug's next call was to Artie. More than any other person Artie's role was extremely important. He dialed Artie's number.

"Hello?"

"Hi Artie, this is Doug. Got a few moments?"

"Sure, anything for you. What's up" Artie asked.

"I spoke briefly with the President last night, he offered whatever help we need to get this going so I will pass along his contacts. Reach out to them and get them moving. We don't have much time as you are aware. We must make Friday happen but before you take any further steps, always, always pray. God will open the doors since He wants this to work.

"Most important is the approvals and cooperation of the communications networks, primarily satellite feeds, downloads, distributions to network and local stations. The Administration's team will make it happen because God will make it happen. Remember that and give Him the Glory when you see it playing out before your eyes.

"Mr. Randall will be in touch about social media. I believe he is on board and will run with whatever you assign him. Load him up and be sure to have him keep things international.

"I just spoke to Charlie Randall; he is on his way over as we speak. I better get going. Blessings to you Pastor."

Doug sat back in his office chair and with tears streaming down his cheeks offered praise to God for using him as a vessel at this appointed moment of time.

~~~

Jon had an early afternoon appointment with the Paddington family at the church. Their patriarch, Harrison Kelsey Paddington was the ailing eighty-something church member whom Jon had visited in the hospital last week. It was unfortunate the dear man had passed away last-night and the family wanted Jon to handle the funeral. It was scheduled for next week to allow out of town relatives time to arrive. The day was set for Tuesday at 10 AM and Jon was to gather with the family on Monday morning to review final arrangements. Until then Jon made himself available to any family member who would like counseling or family prayers. To Jon's astonishment, the whole family declined counseling and did not want any prayers.

This troubled Jon because he was now aware of the importance of prayer in times like these but also it appeared none of the family had been saved. Jon knew he had his work cut out for him in his funeral message Tuesday. How incredibly sad their eyes are blinded and how lost they were without the hope of Jesus in their life.

12

Wednesday - Preparations

Jon was so looking forward to his new nightly dreams that he could hardly close his eyes with an overabundance of expectation and excitement filling his soul. Like a child on Christmas Eve his efforts at sleep were anxious and sporadic but soon, by sheer exhaustion he drifted off to sleep. The dream that ensued did not disappoint.

It began very simply and grew from one ribbon to a tapestry of every color element that could be absorbed by brain. As I was enjoying the evolution of the event, the most perfect harmonics* of voices singing permeated my ears. The sheer joy of singing and harmony was more than I could endure, and I began sobbing tears of utter joy at the magnificence of what was before me. After what seemed to be hours of this all-absorbing blessing, my emotions of gratitude and thanksgiving were bursting at the seams, and I could not take any more lest I explode.

6:20 AM. Notes and smiles. Deep, restful sleep soon overwhelmed an exhausted soul.

~~~

Artie was the first one to interrupt Doug's morning prayer. "The communications network that will originate at the First Presbyterian Church of Arlington are just about set and should be ready tomorrow evening for a trial run.

"Doug, I can't begin to describe how all this is setting up. When something needs to be addressed a person becomes available and in moments the problem is solved. Doug, these are not incidental blips, they are the type of boulders that would indefinitely delay a project of this magnitude and the boulder just vanishes into paving material, the project moves on. I have seen this time and again and I am amazed."

"Just keep up the miracles Artie. We need them. I told you prayer before your action would clear the way." Doug reassured. "Is there anything I can do to help?"

"Yeah, just one thing. Get Charlie Randall out of my hair. I cannot keep up with his progress on social media. His boulders are crumbling before him, and he is so excited he keeps the whole office in stitches laughing so hard. I must hand it to him. I thought he would need a lot of baby-sitting, but he just seems to know what to do and gets it done. He is way ahead of me and seems to have this one solved."

"I sensed he was our man to handle social media. Keep it going Artie."

~~~

Charlie decided to give Doug a call this morning since the social media tasks seem to be wrapping up. "Hi Doug, it's me Charlie, just checking back in to see if there is anything else I should be doing today."

"Hi, Charlie. Good to hear from you. I just talked to Artie a few moments ago and he says you are knocking social media off our list. Great job. I do have something for you. I have not heard from Pastor Jon since Monday. Would you mind swinging by his place and see how he and Rose are doing?"

"Sure Doug, I'm not far from his home. I'll double back to you later. Take care."

"Thanks Charlie. Blessings to you."

~~~

Charlie settled into the local traffic as he made his way over to the Wyatt home. There Jon met Charlie at the door and, after collegial welcoming, headed toward the kitchen table. The kitchen table seemed to be the appropriate location to comfortably sit, sip coffee, and share what is going on in their lives.

Charlie jumped in first explaining the social media advances. "Well over five million people have seen Jon's sermon from Sunday. They are all hearing about the upcoming broadcast this Friday and are inviting others to share the video and invite more to view the broadcast. The word is spreading like wildfire. "My mind cannot absorb how this is taking off." "

Jon heard all this, with a knowing smile and a nod here and there. For some reason he seemed to be well ahead of Charlie and his good news. Then Jon explained the series of dreams that he was having the past few nights. Charlie was spellbound as he jotted down notes of his visions. When he finished, we both sat there in stunned silence. Charlie was speechless and numb. Jon just smiled.

Jon could tell from his expression that he had not made a commitment to Christ, or rather he sensed it in his soul. "Charlie, who do you say Jesus is?"

The question cut him to the quick and he didn't have an answer for Jon. As he stuttered, Jon answered for Charlie, "He is the lover of your soul, the beginning and end, your healer and provider, the

Son of God, your savior and redeemer. Are you familiar with those words?"

"Er, yes. They are English and I understand them." Although the exact meaning of a couple of terms did throw Charlie for a loop as he attempted to recover from Jon's questioning.

"Charlie, I need to ask you If you are born again? Have you apologized to Jesus for your sins and asked Him to forgive you? Will you receive Him to be Lord in your life?"

These questions sent Charlie's head spinning even more and he looked at his wrist, where a watch might have been worn and said "Gee, look at the time, I really have to get going. It was so nice to visit with you this morning and like I said, I got to meet someone in a few minutes. Bye" and was out the door.

Charlie's heart was pounding as he jumped into his car and backed down the driveway. He wanted to stay but was too afraid to commit. "Afterall, I have plenty of time to make such decisions and am not going to get cornered by Jon into making any pledge or oath or such."

After his quick escape, Charlie just drove round Arlington, thinking circular thoughts about Jon's intrusion into his personal matters. He ended up at Arlington Cemetery where he thought he could find solitude and could roll over in his mind what Jon spoken about.

He was near one of the endless rows of crosses when a worker appeared out of nowhere who asked him if he had any relatives in the cemetery. "Oh, maybe an uncle or so going back a few generations."

"That's fine, but you seem very absorbed in your thoughts, anything I can do to help?" said the worker.

"Yeah, I have a question. Is this all there is?" Charlie asked sarcastically hoping to get an answer that he could easily reject.

"Now that's a very deep question. Reality is what we see. What we don't see can also be reality. Such as I have a wallet in my back pocket that you cannot see, yet it is still very real. The Good Book quotes Jesus as saying, *"I will go and prepare a place for you, if this were not so I would have told you."* All it takes is a little faith to assume Jesus will do as he says. Either he is right or wrong. Which would you wish to be the truth?"

Charlie replied, "I would guess it would be the best answer to say he would make a place for us."

"You have answered your question. The reality beyond what you see only requires a little faith. With that, the rest is easy. Have yourself a great day Charlie." the worker replied as he walked away.

Charlie sat on the ground and thought long and hard as to what the worker had said. After a few minutes it occurred to him that he never introduced himself to the worker "so how did he know my name?" Charlie spun around but the worker was gone.

~~~

By this time Sophia had been tapping into just about every intercessor group in the country and half the world. The network she pulled together could only have been the result of a miracle. She knew someone who knew someone who knows someone and so it went. The vision of prayerful intercession for all things small, large, and impossible went up like incense to the heavens. Gratitude and thanksgiving were offered for what God was doing and it multiplied the efforts of the faithful. Friday's broadcast will be going out into the entire world, and it is in keeping with the desire and will of the Almighty. Sophia proudly proclaimed the verse from Matthew 24:14 *"And this gospel of the kingdom will be preached in the whole world as a testimony to all nations, and then the end will come."*

13

Thursday—Final Details / Charlie's Dilemma

As Jon drifted off to sleep shortly after midnight, he was anticipating another dream but could not imagine or conceive a continuation of the dream's progression. He was mistaken.

First was floating aimlessly, then a dancing ribbon changing in colors soon to be joined by an incredible tapestry of more ribbons, colors, and hues. Right after that came the harmonics of incredibly beautiful music of voices singing joyously. Jon reminded himself of the overwhelming emotions he felt last time and again he broke into a joyful sobbing when his mind took in what happened next. From behind and below came wave after wave of similar tapestries flying past him upwards in front of him. The music changed to differing styles all unique and just as enveloping, amplified colors far surpassing their predecessors in brilliance and dominance. The surging numbers of tapestries carried me along with their energy at a frightening speed all of us twisting, turning, spiraling, flying, accelerating upward heading toward a distant...

6:20 AM. Jon was exhilarated at his dream but disappointed in how it ended. What were we headed towards? How soon would we get there? Jon had no answers, so he jotted down his recollections, rolled over and replayed the dream over and over in his mind until he drifted off to sleep.

~~~

Doug was in his office early going over his voicemails when he got a report from Charlie that floored him. Over three-hundred million views of Pastor Wyatt's sermon have been seen on social media outlets carrying his message. "Praise the Lord!" shouted Doug at the good news.

His next message was from Sophia who reported feedback from the communist nation intercessors. Apparently, their governments are getting wind of the upcoming broadcast and plans are being laid to circumvent the people's ability to hear Pastor Wyatt. The full impact cannot yet be discerned but the prayer warriors are adding fasting to their efforts to breakthrough these obstacles.

Lastly was a call from Arnie. His report was of good news. Everything is in place from a network broadcasting perspective. Everything is all set for tomorrow's epic event. Although this would appear as excellent news, Doug had an ominous sense of despair.

"Hello?"

"Hi Arnie, this is Doug. I just got your message, and I am a bit concerned. Just before your message was one from Sophia. The intercessor network is reporting strong resistance from some communist countries in their efforts to stop our broadcast. What are you hearing?"

"I have heard of some rumblings to that effect. I have top-notch guys working on it as we speak. Hopefully, it will get resolved."

"What is your backup plan if they don't?" asked Doug, wishing there was a good answer.

"Don't have one yet but I am working on it." Artie added.

Doug replied, "I'm not sure if it would even be possible, but I was having a dream last night about my dad. In the fifties and sixties, he was an avid ham operator. He used to tell me about all his contacts around the world he could reach every night. That got me thinking. Can the short-wave operators around the world pull in Pastor Wyatt's message? And secondly, can they push it on over the local airways?"

"I see where you are going. Sounds like a Plan B. I will add the ham operators to our network and work out the details. God will get this done. Make sure Jon is at his church for a test session today at noon. Doug, I must admit, as we sat in your office Monday morning, I had no confidence in this getting off the ground. But here we are, three days later, a day ahead of time, and we are nailing down the final details of this impossible effort. I am beyond amazed."

"Arnie, you should be. What you are witnessing is truly a God thing. His will is making this happen, not your efforts, not mine, not Pastor Wyatt's. We are all vessels here to accomplish His greater work."

Doug's next call was to Sophia. "Hi, Sophia, this is Doug."

"His Pastor, did you get my voice mail?"

"Yes, I did. Seems to me we are in a position where we cannot do much in those areas of the world in communist control. But as you often have said, "When we cannot, God can." Do you have anything further?"

"Indeed, I do. The intercessors have been hammering away at those strongholds, intercessors from across the whole world, are thanking and praising God for doing what we cannot. Opening the doors for God to act. It's a done deal, all you need is faith, and the mountain will be flung into the sea."

"Sophia, you are so right. I will rest on your and HIs assurance. Bye."

"Bye to you, too. Blessings."

Doug's last call was to Charlie Randall. "Hi, Charlie, Doug here. How are you doing?"

"Great, Pastor Kucher. Did you get my voicemail?"

"Yes, I did. It's amazing. Your social media postings have helped in unimaginable ways. People over all the earth are asking to hear more of Pastor Wyatt's message. Their demand is making it easier for our technical crew to move through red tape and get this set-up. That and, of course, God."

"Your comments are appreciated but my portion consisted of pressing a few keyboard buttons, uploading a video with comments, and sitting back watching as this takes off. It must be God because I have never seen anything like this take off so rapidly at warp speed." Charlie had to admit something besides his meager efforts is behind the ultra-viral takeoff of his postings. This caught Charlie by surprise that he could even think of denying his contribution while giving credit to God. "It leads me to believe there is something to what all these 'religious' people are saying. That 'something' is something I need to consider, and soon."

~~

The sound checks and video check at First Presbyterian Church of Arlington went so smoothly and without any glitches that the crew began wrapping up the trial just as Doug entered the church.

"Hi Jon." Doug said.

"Hi Pastor Kucher. I'm glad you were able to stop by. Your physical support means so much to me."

"Pastor Wyatt, I wouldn't miss this movement of God for anything. You see, the day you just happened to catch me leaving my church last week was serendipitous. I intended to leave for the gym earlier, but things kept getting in my way, delaying my leaving, right up to the moment we met. Your dreams intrigued me to no end. You were a pastor, but about as green as they come and hardly ever at your age in life. I was happy to get you pointed in the right direction but the dreams you described to me are dreams that I have never even thought possible. Yet you happened upon my door, asking my advice. I was but a simple Christian doing as I have been taught led by the Holy Spirit.

"After seeing you for our short visit, I had to see if my advice to you was well taken so I showed up at your church last Sunday and was simply blown away. The message you gave was entirely inspired by God and I was impressed to take that message a far as I could humanly achieve. You have been called and qualified to preach a message, the message that God wants the world to hear. I am incredibly humbled to be a small part of that. Thank you, Jon, for picking up that mantle."

"I'm humbled as well to be in God's favor and pray I will not disappoint Him. "Jon replied.

"God is good." Doug replied, paused, and then added: "I also want to encourage you on your message for tomorrow. Although you will be broadcast world-wide, I just want you to be talking to the people in your home church. Keep your focus on them and you should not have any problem."

"Thanks, Doug. I am just planning on delivering the same message with only a couple of changes. The Lord knows I have been praying the message will be well presented using His words and not mine. What time do you want Rose and me to be here tomorrow, around ten?"

"Sure, that would be perfect. There will be a lot of last-minute details to check and resolve but your being here at ten would work out fine." Doug said "And I will be praying for you along with thousands of intercessors. Nothing should go wrong."

"OK Doug. See you in the morning."

"You too, Jon."

As Jon turned to leave, he spotted Jason and Rose, the newly engaged couple Jon had met with last week. They were early for their final counseling session, but it was fortunate because the session completely slipped Jon's mind.

"Oh, I am glad we caught you here early," explained Jason, "we have a few other appointments this afternoon and hoped we could meet right away. Do you mind?"

"Why no. Right 'now' would be perfect. Come on back to my office." Jon said as he led the couple away. After they were seated Jon opened: "Well, a week has gone by any you two are still together I see."

"Yes sir!" said Rose "We are just about to set the date and we want to tell our folks first then clear it with you."

"Very good. Have you had a chance to discuss the compatibility assessment I gave you last week?"

"Yes, Pastor Wyatt, we have." said Jason, smiling widely at his future bride. "We both discussed all the topics, and we are in total agreement with the assessment. Our score puts us in the top 2%." He added proudly.

"I'm proud you two found each other. Now I have an important question for you two – where is your faith? Are you two born again?" They sheepishly smiled at each other and added they were not.

That was just the opening Jon needed. "The chances of your marriage surviving well into your eighties significantly improves when you both are equally yoked spiritually. That is, both of you having the same faith, believing the way. Having Jesus in your lives will not avoid life's pitfalls and pain but it will see you through the tough times and keep you close. Would you like to begin your life together joined in faith, believing spiritually the same way?"

They both said in unison "Sure we do!"

"Then repeat after me..." and Jon led them in the sinner's prayer, and both became saved, born-again into the family of God.

"One last thing." Jon interjected as they were getting ready to leave. "I am delivering a message tomorrow at noon here at the church. I would be most please if you both could be here. I guarantee you will not be disappointed. Can you both make it?"

"Yes, Pastor Wyatt, we would both love to be there. See you then." Jason told Jon.

"Great. See you there."

~~~

Jon spent the rest of the day practicing his sermon. Each time it came out to forty-six minutes, give, or take a minute. Rose was busy arranging some refreshments for the church after the broadcast.

Artie worked on the shortwave crowd, expanding the network, and enlisted everyone he met to spread the word giving the technical aspects of getting the signal and what to do with it locally. All the guys seemed to be talking the same language as Artie, so things went smoothly. Many ham enthusiasts offered to bring Artie along as a novice after the broadcast.

Sophia kept passing along messages for the intercessors as they took direct aim at the political leaders in the communist countries to agree on allowing the broadcast. Prayers for Jon were also requested but for the most part the request was already being answered.

Doug went back to his office, relaxed in his Bible reading for the day, and eventually took a nap knowing things were running smoothly for tomorrow's epic event.

Charlie spent the afternoon wandering Arlington Cemetery, hoping to see the worker again and half wishing he wouldn't. A ball of confusion was racing around Charlie's head as he tried to sort out his resistance to coming to the Lord. He couldn't come up with an answer, so he decided to face it again on Friday.

14

Friday – Final Details

Jon awoke early and prayed, "Lord, you called me to this for your reasons. I am your vessel, please give me the strength of conviction, the clarity of mind, the vision of purpose, and the voice of your words. Allow me to reach those souls with their last chance to reach all of humanity. Amen." With that, Jon prepared for this day with a purpose he had never known.

~~~

Doug arose early, well before dawn, to prepare for the day. He was anxious yet trusting in the preparations that have been laid, all with the blessing and encouragement from God that his efforts were in perfect alignment of God's desire. The number "12" came to his mind straight out of the blue. God's number of completeness, wholeness. Then he realized it was just 12 days ago that Jon's dreams began. It was twelve months ago to the day that Doug decided to retire from his pastorship but was convinced by the elders of his church to remain for one last year. And then he heard that still, small voice in his ear whisper it was twelve years ago that Doug prayed with a passion he never felt before to bring meaning to his service to the Lord, and that the last twelve years was his training in faith and in works for this very moment in time. Wave after wave of emotions fell over Doug as he recalled time after time that God blessed him in his dedication to his flock and his mission in life.

~~~

Ten o'clock arrived quickly as every-one gathered early at the First Presbyterian Church of Arlington. The technical crew were busy double checking the endless tasks of preparation needed for such an epic event. Parishioners were standing in line for a couple of hours hoping to get a place inside for the message. Pastor Wyatt was in his study along with Rose, Doug, and a couple of elders.

Doug was the first to spot Charlie as he entered the study. "Hi Charlie, I am glad to see you here."

"I wouldn't miss this for the world." he nervously blurted out. Here was the last place Charlie wanted to be, but something convinced him to at least stop by and see how the endgame of this monumental effort turns out. Sensing that the others in the room were unaware of his turmoil Charlie settled into an overstuffed leather chair and tried to look invisible.

Artie and Sophia arrived shortly and bid hello and blessings and hugs to Jon and Rose.

At ten-thirty the crowd was let into the church where they were all seated with nervous energy anticipating a movement of the Lord. Every seat was taken. The buzz of excited conversation added to the palpable tension gripping the crowd.

Around eleven thirty the choir began singing praise and worship songs. It seemed to Charlie like an opening act for Jon as Charlie was amused at the similarities of a rock concert and was totally clueless as to the songs' significance. Pastor Kucher sensed the correct moment and offered a prayer of spiritual covering for Jon in the delivery of his message and a prayer of protection for the network of technical matters surrounding the broadcast and everything perform as expected in getting Jon's message out without interruptions, complications, or technical difficulties. Everyone said Amen at the conclusion of the prayers, and all tried to hide their nervous smiles. Jon had a demeanor Charlie had not seen, part confidence and determination and part uncertain as to his ability to perform. Charlie checked it off as nerves and went to find his seat as did the others leaving Jon alone with his thoughts waiting for the cue from Doug to enter the sanctuary.

15

Worldwide

The few brief moments between Doug leaving his office and Doug introducing Jon seemed like an eternity. Demonic forces showered lies upon lies against Jon. He was unworthy, he was not qualified, he will be an embarrassment to his family, his church, his friends, and his nation. He will trip when he enters, he will get the hiccups, he will lose his place in the sermon, he will spill water all over his papers because of his nerves. He will omit the important parts and over-emphasize the unimportant ones. People will get up and run out of the church, the transmission of the broadcast will be problematic and a distraction to his message. Jon is too short, he is too tall, his hair is unkempt, his shoelace is undone, his zipper is down, your zipper is up but not really – check again, Rose left some lipstick on his cheek and which door do I go through, Doug will get mad at him, Artie will get mad at him, Sophia will get mad at him, Rose will be ashamed of him. He may have to commit suicide after this whole thing is over. When will it be over? When will Doug introduce me? Why is my mouth so dry? Why is my tongue too big to speak properly? What is my name again?

"... my honor to introduce my dear friend, Pastor Jon Wyatt, from this, the First Presbyterian Church of Arlington."

Polite applause greeted Jon as he made his way to the Podium. It settled him to see familiar faces sitting in the pews and the comfortable ambiance of First Presbyterian. Aside from three or four cameramen and a bank of lights, Jon was in familiar territory and his anxiety level waned.

He glanced to the usual spot where Rose sat every Sunday. There he found his beautiful bride seated next to Pastor Kucher, Sophia, Artie, and then Charlie.

He began, "This might be your last chance. Please hear me. (pause) *'For God so loved the world that he gave his only begotten son, that whosoever believes in Him shall not perish but have everlasting life.'* (pause) John 3:16, perhaps the most quoted verse in scripture. Virtually everyone has heard this verse, but how many really know and understand this verse? It is the key that unlocks my eternity, and it can unlock yours. Twelve days ago, I did not 'know' this verse and I was a pastor. I am ashamed that I didn't, but God's grace covered that. He chose me of all people to receive a vision in the form of dreams. A series of dreams defining my role in God's plan for his people. During those dreams, God opened my eyes and this servant, Pastor Doug Kucher, sitting next to my wife Rose, led me to confess my sins, to thank Jesus for paying the price for my sins on the cross, and to acknowledge Jesus as my Lord and Savior.

"I have heard that well over 300 million people have listened to my sermon from last Sunday. I am humbled at this interest, and I dare say much of it needs to be repeated for those watching or listening around the world for the first time.

"The dreams were filled with imagery about an event in time that has been predicted and prophesized since the early Biblical writings. Please follow me as I recount those dreams.

"The first dream, a week ago Monday morning as my notes reflect: *Everything seemed slightly out of focus, I'm standing in a field stretching far off to the horizon. The landscape is generally flat with long gentle slopes, not really hills. Straight in front of me in the far distance is a wall. At least that is what I would guess to call it, yes, it appears to be a wall.*

"The next night, the dream repeated with slight changes:

"Everything seems a bit clearer this time. I'm standing in a vast field covered with a green carpet of ankle-high seedlings and it feels like a warm spring afternoon. There is that red wall again and I expect it is made from bricks even though it is still far away." Both nights the time on my digital clock was 3:16 AM when I woke up.

"Wednesday and Thursday morning dreams were each similar but with each the details changed. Wednesday the seedlings grew to knee-high, the sun was bright and warming the day while two workers were standing at a distance and were just waiting. In Thursday's dream I found I was walking through a wheat field easily identifiable by the stalks and seeds, the weather was hotter like a mid-summer day and a slight breeze wafted past me from behind. The sky was hazy, the workers were still waiting, and I began hearing a bizarre knocking sound in my head, quite out of place in a wheat field. Again, in each dream the wall was either growing larger or growing nearer or both and was increasingly ominous and I awoke each morning at 3:16 AM.

"Friday morning's dream:

"The dream reappeared as vividly as before. Perhaps even more so as the scene surrounding me projected a higher dimension of detail, the individual stalks of wheat, now grown to waist high, remained visible trailing off into the distance as if Jon's vision improved greatly beyond a mere 20/20 level. The wall was moving closer, and the redness appeared

more of a maroon, darker than before. The size of the wall was at least hundreds of feet tall rising majestically into the air. Its distance was still not discernable but nearer. The two workers were starting to prepare for their work, getting out supplies and they could be heard talking to each other though not loud enough to understand their conversation. They were wearing baggy clothing and wide brimmed hats to keep the sun off. Each wore heavy gloves and work boots. The sky was still hazy, but clouds were beginning to billow upwards toward the heavens and the wind freshened to a stiff breeze, again from behind. The stirring of the air brought with it dusty or perhaps musty odors typical of the rural setting. The heat was building, and a sweat started to drench my shirt. It's a bit bizarre, but I find myself saying these words aloud and I hear them as if spoken by a deeper voice. I start walking in the direction of the wall, again with the workers on my left, and discover3d a railroad bed crossing the field with a few open-bin rail cars behind me. Strange that I hadn't noticed them before. I decide, although I am not sure why, to follow the rail path heading toward the wall. As I walk, I can hear my footsteps, my steady breathing, and this incessant knocking inside my head. I wish it would stop! 3:16AM

"You can see the dreams are more vivid, detailed with symbology, and ominous in their events. It was on the afternoon of this day that I met Pastor Kucher, the conversation led to the salvation of my soul and altered my destiny. The mystery of 3:16 AM was revealed: my name is Jon, a variation of John, J-O-H-N, put with the time and you get John 3:16 which also points to my birthdate of March 16th. The time after each dream clearly indicates the dream was meant for me and both reference the opening verse of my sermon today. In my Sunday sermon I recounted my Saturday morning dream that I will repeat again:

"*"I realize I am in the dream again but there is chaos everywhere. The wind is howling from behind me with a wail I have never heard before and it smells of burning weeds that stings my nostrils. Ash is flying past me with bits of harvested wheat stalks as if blown by a tornado. The two workers were furiously swinging their sickles carving great swaths in the ripened wheat. The severed stalks laden with kernels flew into the air and were separated by the wind into stalks and kernels. Unexpectedly, the stalks settled to the ground and were instantly consumed by fire while the kernels were blown upward, high into the air and out of sight. This harvesting was an instantaneous and endless process performed by the workers laboring, in their furor, to gather the entire harvest. I thought to myself: "Why are there not more workers?*

"The sky was billowing with storm clouds growing darker by the second as if to unload their torrent upon the furious activity in the field. The rail cars, filled with grain from previous harvests were rolling on the tracks, gathering speed, careening toward a small door in the wall. The wall. THE WALL! The wall, that a day earlier seemed so far away was nearly upon the field. It reached higher in the air than the approaching storm clouds. Nothing could go over it or around it. Its momentum would not be stopped as it moved towards the field in front of me and the storms fury approached from the rear creating a cataclysm of opposing irresistible forces. Torrents of rain, hail and lightning ripped loose from the sky immediately soaking me the workers, and the field. My thoughts were in conflict; self-preservation in the face of such adversity or throw myself into a final frenzy of harvesting. Out of nowhere, one of the workers disappeared. I raced to join in the harvest grabbing his sickle and began to cut giant swaths in the ripened wheat. The incessant downpour and the approaching wall were inconsequential in my desire to swing the sickle

one more time, one more time. TIME! That wall represents time! Insatiably moving forward, never ceasing, stopping, or waiting. The wall of time approaching, marching to the beat of a second-long metronome. Closer, closer, closer every second the wall trampled the field directly in its path. It was the last race against time I was waging as the wall was gaining on me. I turned away from the approaching monolith to concentrate on the harvest. My back ached and my arms screamed for rest - one more swing, one more time. The wall was almost upon me when it slowed to a crawl allowing me to harvest ever more wheat. One more swing, one more time, one more swing, one more swing, one more swing, one mo...

    (Pause) What a series of dreams. Each one building on the other. From one to the next we can see that time has elapsed in the stages of the wheat encompassing a harvest but also the approaching wall. The changing weather and increased heat all were efforts to stymie the workers and represents the efforts of the enemy to circumvent God's plan. The train of wheat represents past harvests barreling into the wall's narrow gate. Wheat signifies mankind, the harvest is the separation of the good parts, the wheat kernels from the useless parts, the chaff. The kernels are saved, and the chaff is burned. The workers are the Christians doing their best to bring in the harvest of souls before the approaching wall dictates when the harvest must stop. What is the authority that allows the wall to bring an end to the harvest? Simply, its God's timing. He alone establishes the time and when it's up, either individually or collectively during the end times it over and done. Period. No exceptions. We can only discern the season for harvesting.

    "What happened to the worker who suddenly went missing in the Friday dream? There is an answer for in Matthew 24:40, *"Two men will be in the field, one will be taken and the other left."* The worker was taken. What does this mean? Let me tell you the continuing series of dreams that I had starting with last Sunday morning:

"Floating. The word choice was a poor one since it only described about a tenth of what I am feeling. Floating*, with no weight or a sense of "up" or origination or destination. Just floating. Any stress that was once in my body has long since dissipated. Muscles have yielded and relaxed. My eyes naturally close but also naturally open without expectation of seeing. There was light but it was coming from all directions much like when you fly through a cloud. I noticed nothing familiar with my sense of smell although there is a flowery aroma wafting from nowhere. I felt warmth but not heat as the temperature was ideally perfect No wind and I felt absolute comfort relaxing in and being in this floating. Serenity, peace, no worry as time just vanishes away. Aaahhh!"

"Monday Morning

"The dream of floating had returned just as satisfying and peaceful as the previous night but with a twist. Round about my floating body appeared a ribbon of color, white at first, then it changed to bright blue, then to a deep red, then to brilliant yellow, earthly green, and on and on through all the colors of the rainbow. Then it repeated the process at a quicker tempo. Then again at a slower rate. It was mesmerizingly beautiful as it completely enveloped my attention!'

"Tuesday Morning:

"The dream began the same as Sunday morning but changed again to the ribbon of my dream on Monday but then took on a whole new dimension with multiple ribbons twirling about my body flashing more colors than could ever be conceived. The ribbons would separate and then weave in and out forming a kaleidoscope of color impossible to imagine. The weaves and spinning of the ribbons vacillated in speed, rhythm, motion, and texture. It was such an entertaining and giddy spectacle I wished it to never end!"

"Wednesday Morning:

"It began very simply and grew from one ribbon to a tapestry of every color element that could be absorbed my brain. As I was enjoying the evolution of the event the most perfect harmonics of voices singing permeated my ears. The sheer joy of singing and harmony was more than I could endure, and I began sobbing tears of utter joy at the magnificence of what was before me. After what seemed to be hours of this all-absorbing blessing, my emotions of gratitude and thanksgiving were bursting at the seams, and I could not take any more lest I explode!"

"And yesterday morning:

"First was floating aimlessly, then a dancing ribbon changing in colors soon to be joined by an incredible tapestry of more ribbons, colors, and hues. Right after that came the harmonics of incredibly beautiful music of voices singing joyously. Jon reminded himself of the overwhelming emotions he felt last time and again he broke into a joyful sobbing when his mind took in what happened next. From behind and below came wave after wave of similar tapestries flying past him upwards in front of him. The music changed to differing styles all unique and just as enveloping, amplified colors far surpassing their predecessors in brilliance and dominance. The surging numbers of tapestries carried me along with their energy at a frightening speed all of us twisting, turning, spiraling, flying, accelerating upward heading toward a distant ...!

"Lastly, my dream earlier this morning:

"As I was enthralled in my visions and rapt in my sensations, wishing to never deviate from my destiny of fellowship within the brethren, I happened to catch out of the corner of my eye a single soul. That single *soul was not floating, nor colorful; lacked any beauty emanating in song, was dark, lifeless, lost, and suffering in extreme anxiety and agony.*

"In a moment's breath, I reached out to touch this soul and with this act of empathy I instantly became aware of a multitude of souls so vast I could not fathom their number. All hopeless in their demeanor. My joy and expectations evaporated as I asked one: why such sorrow?" 'Because we were unaware and had chosen the wrong path, hesitated too long. We chose not to believe."

"Imploring aloud, I begged 'please God, give them one last chance.' My plea echoed into the vast sea of indifference, and I heard, not so much as with my ears but with my whole being: **EVEN THOUGH THEY DO NOT DESERVE ANTHER CHANCE I WILL GRANT EACH SOUL ONE LAST OPPORTUNITY AND ANTICIPATE THEY WILL ACCEPT MY GIFT OF SALVATION.'** *The voice of all Authority had spoken.*

"The time, I understood without looking was 6:20 AM. John 6:20, Jesus is speaking, and the verse reads: 'It is I, don't be afraid.'

"'It is I, do not be afraid.' And the worker vanished, 'It is I, do not be afraid.' And one last chance.

"The dreams I received over the past twelve nights shows how we are born, witness the seedlings, grow, and ripen with passage of time and ultimately are harvested whether by circumstances of life or at the end of the age. We become the wheat or the chaff by our own decision. Once on the other side of the wall, when our time has expired, and we have been fortunate to accept Jesus' gift of salvation, we will then be among those brethren ascending to heaven with joy overflowing in grateful appreciation. Otherwise, well, not so good.

"Dithering can be catastrophic. As I said at the beginning of this address: Listen. This may be your last chance. No one knows the time of our last breath. You may walk outside after my message and be hit by a car, have a sudden heart attack, or die of a massive stroke. If you do not know Jesus, if you have not given your life to the King of Kings, if you have not asked him to forgive your sins, then you must, with all the faith and trust you have, repeat this prayer after me:

"Jesus, I believe you are the Son of the Living God."

People repeated.

"And that I am sorry that I am a sinner in need of forgiveness."

People repeated.

"Please forgive me of my sins, come in, and become Lord of my Life."

People repeated.

"Thank you and Amen." People again repeated.

"Those of you who repeated this prayer with honesty and sincerity, now have the assurance that you will be with Jesus in heaven, your destiny has instantly changed in unimaginable ways, and spiritually you have been reborn. Get a Bible and read it. Find a church where you can fellowship and grow in your faith. Welcome to the family of God! Thank you for listening to my story and may God richly bless you."

An outpouring of applause began in the worship hall followed by a few praise hymns from the choir and the broadcast ended.

16

In A Twinkling

Jon was greatly relieved the broadcast was over. Rose came over to him at the podium and gave him a huge hug that nearly knocked Jon over. Doug Kucher had a huge smile on his face and shook Jon's hand so hard it nearly took Jon's arm off. Sophia just stood in front of her chair and was praising the Lord as tears streamed down her face. Charlie came over to talk to Jon and waited for the world's longest handshake to end when he said to Jon "I want you to know that I said that prayer and I am so hap"

At that moment, between the two p's in 'happy', Charlie saw a twinkling in Rose's eye, and it happened. A brilliant flash of light coming from nowhere and everywhere. The light was intense yet not blinding.

Now here is where Jon was blessed by the Lord. For Jon, the world's time nearly stood still as he looked at the gathered souls within his church: Jerry and Betty, Bennie, Doug and Sophia and Artie, Jason and Rose, the sound technicians and the camera men including Larry and Tim, the guys from the diner, the church ladies and their husbands, the elders, and the deacons. Every one of them were disappearing and starting to float upwards toward the ceiling. Around each soul appeared a white ribbon vividly turned to a dazzling, different color and changed again to another color as the ribbons danced around each soul entwining with other ribbons as they started their ascent. Jon felt himself losing his footing as he started to rise, when he noticed Charlie standing before him. Jon looked puzzled at Charlie wondering why Charlie was not joining the rest of the brethren. There was a smile on Charlie's face and lastly, he too began disappearing as a white ribbon appeared around him. In an instant, time resumed for Jon and the entire collection of saved souls, including the last one, Charlie, disappeared through the church roof flying toward heaven, racing to meet JESUS.

The same scenario repeated in the same instant of time all across America, Europe and the rest of the world. As all the souls were rising, Jesus shouted to his chosen, "**Welcome! Welcome Home My Brethren! Welcome!**"

In a twinkling, once only seen in Rose's eye, the rapture abruptly and decisively concluded. What remained was chaff.

Epilogue

A few final thoughts .... I cannot imagine standing in a crowd watching the broadcast of Jon Wyatt's worldwide message with a cynical smirk on my face, disbelieving all that "Christianity" stuff, smug in my indifference. When instantly most of the people surrounding me unbelievably vanished. How would those remaining justify in their mind the stupidity of their decision? Perhaps someone sent you this book and you have the same attitude. How would you justify remaining when many-to-most of your peers were raptured?

Dithering can be catastrophic. The prophesies of which Jon spoke will manifest at some point. The Wall of time one day will be upon you, it will just be too late. Perhaps it will be you when your time has come, "After This" you will face the judgement. And you must answer the question, "Are you wheat or chaff?"

*One note for those who seem perplexed at the whole ribbon thing going on in the later chapters, I must admit I took a certain "author's license" to add a feeling of splendor to those being taken away. Surely that experience must be the most exceptional trip up to the heavens and I felt a need to add drama to the occasion even though there is no scriptural reference to floating, ribbons, or harmonic music. As the song says, 'I can only imagine', but the ascension of souls during the rapture is beyond what my words can express, or my mind begin to imagine. I apologize if I have disappointed in those expressions.

Please pass this book along to someone else with a need to contemplate their destiny. Perhaps that lonely soul will one day rejoice as he or she races toward heaven.

Let me know your thoughts at my email address:

r.s.johnson.author@gmail.com

and thank you for reading my book.

A special thank you to Larry Doel, Doug Peet, and Tim Suddreth for each donating their precious time to give me valuable feedback on my manuscript. Humbly, it was received, and greatly appreciated!!

Lastly, a huge thank you to my wife, Cindy, who continues to support my literary endeavors. She inspired me to make that "great decision" after dithering in my life for far too long. She keeps me grounded and focused on what is important in life, she forgives generously and loves unconditionally. To that, I aspire.

About the author

"In A Twinkling" is the second literary work conceived by God and revealed in dreams to this author. His first book, "After This" was similarly inspired through several dreams encouraging him to become an author and then gave the inspiration for the content of both books.

Randall began his writing after retiring from a corporate career of over 35 years. His earlier life was filled with full-time work, raising four sons, while performing the constant maintenance on a 1940's cape-style home. His early life was spent growing up in Michigan and pulling for the Spartans at MSU while earning his bachelor's degree.

Randall and his wife Cynthia met in 1984 while both worked at Eastman Kodak Co., were married two years later, and settled in upstate New York. They have been active in their church throughout their marriage and enjoy traveling, boating, biking, and dining out. The couple have recently become snowbirds and joined a southern church family at Suncoast Cathedral in St. Petersburgh, Florida.

"Praise God from whom all blessings flow!"

CPSIA information can be obtained
at www.ICGtesting.com
Printed in the USA
BVHW040325240422
635121BV00008B/149